# THE

# GRAFTON

# HEIST

Printed in the United States

ISBN: 978-1-950381-06-7

Also by Stephanie Andrews:

Chicago Blue
Diamond White
Solid Gold
Agent Orange

Visit the author at www.stephanieandrewsauthor.com

# THE GRAFTON HEIST

Stephanie Andrews

# 1

A crime was about to take place. Nobody in the lobby of the luxurious Drake Hotel had any idea what was about to happen. When it was over, none would have idea of the outcome. It began with the entrance of a man named John Adams.

The man strode leisurely up the stairs and into the lobby. He removed his sunglasses, folded them and placed them casually into the pocket of his tan linen suit. He looked around the lobby, then made his way across the dark-blue carpet to the long reception desk.

"Good afternoon, Mr. Adams," said the woman on duty. "Having a pleasant day?"

"I am," the man said with a smile. He was average in height and slim, with a handsome head of blond hair and a trim, darker goatee with a smattering of gray. He spoke with a very slight Spanish accent.

"I'm doing very well, thank you...Sharon," he said, leaning forward slightly to read her name tag.

"Is there anything I can help you with?"

He held a red iPhone up in his left hand.

"I'm afraid I haven't been able to reach my wife all afternoon. Her phone goes straight to voicemail." He frowned, "She hasn't left any messages here for me, has she?"

"I'll look for you, sir. Give me just a moment."

"Thank you."

The man looked at the chandeliers as Sharon checked for messages. The lobby was filling up with people checking in before dinner. His attention was caught by an older man who carried a cat in his arms as if it were the most common thing in the world. He watched until the man, and the cat, disappeared into the elevator. After a moment, Sharon turned back to him with an apologetic look.

"I'm afraid I have no messages, sir."

"Hmmm," said the man, a worried look on his face. "I hope—"

He was interrupted by the jangling ring of the phone in his hand. He glanced at it and breathed a sigh of relief. "There she is now."

"Astrid," he said, bringing the phone to his ear, "I was getting worri—"

"Shut up and listen!" The voice was filtered through a computer: flat mechanical, high volume. It was so loud that Sharon, five feet away, froze when she heard it.

"Wait, what—"

"I said shut up. We have your wife."

Sharon looked at the man in alarm as the color drained from his face. He leaned forward and braced himself on the counter with his free hand.

"Is this some kind of joke?"

"This is not a joke, and it's not a game. We have your wife and you will do exactly as we say, is that understood?"

"No, I, I don't understand..." he stuttered, shocked.

A woman's scream erupted from the phone, Sharon and Adams both gasped at the same time.

"Astrid!" the man yelled, drawing looks from other guests in the lobby.

The scream stopped.

"Astrid!" the man yelled again, but it was the computerized voice that answered.

"Are you ready to listen to me, Mr. Adams?"

Adams's eyes were wide with terror. He put his hand over the phone and whispered to Sharon.

"Get me a pen and paper, now!"

A muffled voice came from the phone, which Adams brought quickly back to his ear.

"Yes, yes I hear you. Who are you?"

Sharon placed a complimentary hotel pad and pen on the counter between them.

"It doesn't matter who I am," the voice said. "Only that you do exactly as I say."

Call the hotel manager, the man scribbled across the sheet of paper, and then call 911.

"This is a joke. This can't be happening," he said into the phone. "This can't be real!"

"I assure you it is," said the voice.

Sharon stood rooted to the spot, staring at the message. Adams slammed the flat of his hand down on the counter, making her jump and give a stifled yelp. She looked up to see him pointing at the phones on the wall behind her.

"What could you possible want with my wife and me? We're nobody."

Sharon jumped to the phone and dialed quickly, cupping her hand over the receiver to quiet her voice.

"I disagree," said the mechanical voice. "We've been following you for some time. Surely you are familiar with how this works, given your background and your home country."

"My home country?" asked Adams, perplexed. He looked wildly around the lobby for anything that seemed out of place, as if the villain might be calling from just on the other side of the giant flower arrangement that stood on the center table.

"You know what I mean. A socialite disappears, a demand is made, and if that demand is not met, she is returned in pieces. Do we need to send you some pieces, Mr. Adams?"

"You're disgusting," said Adams. His voice was low now, through gritted teeth. "What the hell do you want?"

"Maybe a few fingers first, just to let you know we are serious?"

A short man in a dark suit rushed through a door behind the counter. He looked around wildly until he saw Sharon, who had hung up the phone and then picked it up again and was now waiting for 911 to answer. She pointed at Adams, and the man rushed over.

"What seems—" He stopped when he saw the look on the man's face, a cross between terror and fierce anger. Adams held a finger to his lips and brought his phone away from his ear, pressing a button with his thumb that put it on speaker. He set the phone on the counter.

"Perhaps we will send you her ring finger, so you can be sure it's her. You would recognize this lovely wedding ring, wouldn't you, with an emerald on either side of the diamond?"

The manager, identified by his name tag as Arthur Bradley, gasped loudly.

"It sounds like I have suitably impressed you, Mr. Adams," said the voice, not realizing who had made the noise. "You have something of value, there at the hotel, in the safe."

"Who the hell are you!" Adams shouted viciously at the phone. All noise in the lobby stopped, every eye turned toward the drama that was unfolding at Reception.

"Do not call the police, or your wife will die. Get me what I want, or she will die. I will call back in five minutes. If you do not answer, your wife will die." Several bystanders heard this last message, and a shocked murmur rolled through the lobby.

Adams looked down at his phone, now silent on the counter. His left knee bent unexpectedly, and he fell to the side like a rag doll, crashing into a woman who had come up to see what was going on. They both fell to the carpet. Bradley heaved himself up onto the counter and swung his legs over, hopping down onto the floor on the other side. He grabbed Adams under one arm while two other men rushed to help. One grabbed Adams's other arm while the other helped the woman to her feet. She was crying, though she seemed uninjured. Adams was breathing heavily, trying to wave the men away.

"I'm fine," he insisted, leaning against the counter. He did not seem fine.

"I've got 911 on the phone, finally," Sharon said, almost shouting in her stress. She held the phone out toward Adams, who looked at it like it was a nuclear bomb.

"Oh my god! Didn't you hear him?" he shouted. "Hang up! Now!!"

Sharon screamed and reflexively slammed the phone down into its cradle.

Adams turned to Bradley. "Where's the manager!" he demanded.

"Sir, I am the manager," said Bradley, trying to show calm. "Could you keep your voice—"

"They have my wife!" Adams shouted. "You want me to keep my voice down?" He was incredulous. "Where's the manager?" he repeated, staring around.

"I am the manager, sir, my name is Arthur Bradley." He instinctively straightened his tie.

"There was a woman, last night, when we checked in."

"That was Miss Alcott. The night manager."

"So you're what, the day manager?"

"I am the general manager, sir, and we've got to call the police."

Adams grabbed the man firmly by the upper arm. His grip was surprisingly strong for someone who seemed so lean.

"I gave the woman, Alcott, something to put in the safe last night."

"Sir—"

"I need it. Right now. A blue box, gold hinges, gold lock. The slip says 'Ackerly' on it, my wife's name. I need it," said Adams again, pushing his face into Bradley's.

"Sir, we've got to call—"

"No police!" Adams shouted at him, flapping his arms in exasperation. "Didn't you hear him? They've got my wife!"

"I don't think—"

"I don't care what you think!"

"The police will call back," said a man standing off to the side. He had short red hair and a strong build. He was one of the men who had helped Adams when he collapsed.

Adams whirled on him.

"Who the fuck are you?"

"O'Brian. Chicago PD. Off duty, but I can help."

"No police!" Adams shouted again. The caller had said no police but here they were already. Adams looked like a man about to die of fright.

The phone next to Sharon rang, and she jumped with a scream.

"Don't answer it," demanded Adams. "Do NOT answer it." He turned back to the red-haired cop. "What are you doing here?" he demanded.

"Picking up friends from out of town for dinner," O'Brian said. "But listen, if you hang up on 911 they'll just call back, and if you don't answer, they'll send a squad car down here. It's protocol."

Adams dug the fingers of both hands into the hair on either side of his head, as if he might squeeze his skull until the stress stopped. There was quiet for a moment.

"Sir," began Bradley, but then the phone rang again,

making them all jump.

"Don't!" said Adams, lunging forward as if he might leap over the counter. Bradley reached out and took him by the arm, but Adams shrugged him off, took a step away, then turned back to him with a new fire in his eyes. He'd made his decision. "The blue box. Go get it. Right now!"

"We have to talk to the police," Bradley continued calmly, still trying to tamp down the noise and fuss in his usually serene lobby. This sort of thing did not happen at The Drake.

"Are you refusing?" demanded Adams. "Because I don't think you can legally do that." He looked over his shoulder at the cop. "It's my property, right? He can't refuse to give me back my property!"

The cop opened his mouth to answer but at that moment Adams's phone rang from its place on the wooden reception counter.

Everyone fell silent.

"It's him," said Adams in a hoarse whisper.

"Let me answer it," said the cop, reaching his hand toward the phone.

"Are you crazy?" Adams clasped his hand onto the man's outstretched wrist.

"Speaker phone, then."

They locked eyes for a moment.

"I can help you," said the cop.

Adams let go of the man's wrist and pushed a button on the phone.

"Mr. Adams?" The computerized voice asked into the hushed lobby. Nobody dared move. Fifteen people or more, rooted to the spot. Their genteel afternoon turned into a news flash.

"I'm here."

"Well, that's good. I thought for a moment you might

refuse to answer. You know what would happen then."

Almost immediately, a woman's scream burst from the tiny speaker.

"Stop it!" yelled Adams. He was leaning over the phone as it lay face up on the counter, his hands pressed flat on either side of it, staring down at it as if he could will himself through the screen.

The screaming stopped.

"Do you have what I want?"

"Yes," said Adams instantly, whipping his head up to lock eyes with Bradley. Bradley looked at the cop, who nodded, and then the manager rushed from the lobby.

"And you didn't call the police?"

"No, of course not."

"Not even a little bit?" teased the voice. "Because it's possible I have people watching the entrance to the hotel. It's possible that if they see any police approaching, they will let me know. Would you like to know what happens then?"

"No police," said Adams, in a voice that he hoped was reassuring. His slight Latin accent had become more pronounced as he became more distressed.

"A black town car will roll up in front of the hotel in two minutes," said the voice. "You will get inside it. You will be taken to a safe location, where you will give me the item and I will give you your wife."

The cop was strongly shaking his head, indicating that this was a very bad idea. He waved his arms back and forth in front of his chest, a universal sign for no way.

"That's crazy," said Adams to the phone.

A door at the back of the reception area clicked open and Bradley came in, carrying a flat blue box the size of a hardcover book.

"Once I get in the car, you'll just kill me," continued Adams, reaching for the box at the same time, but

Bradley held it tight.

"Well, sir, it's your choice. I can only give you my word that I will keep my side of the arrangement. You have no reason to trust me, but you have no options either. I don't play games. Two minutes."

The line went dead.

Adams scooped the phone off the counter. "Wait!" he shouted at it, but it was too late. He turned and looked at the cop.

"What do we do now?"

"The police will be here any minute, and we'll take it from there."

"No," said Adams.

"They have procedures for this."

"No," repeated Adams emphatically.

O'Brian put his hands on his hips and looked at the ceiling, then gave a long exhale.

"We've only got one minute!" said Adams through gritted teeth.

"I'll do it," the cop said. He reached his hand out toward Bradley, who handed him the box across the counter. He turned and started for the door.

"What are you talking about?" asked Adams, bewildered.

"I'll go get in the car, and deliver the—"

"That's crazy," said Adams. He grabbed the man by the elbow and pulled the box out of his hand. "They must know what I look like if they have this planned so well."

"But—"

"And what happens when my wife sees you? You think she's going to play along? She's not an actress or a spy. They are torturing her!"

The words echoed through the lobby. The silence that followed was broken by the sound of a horn outside the lobby doors. The two men looked at each other, both

9

knowing the horn was the pick-up car.

"Follow me," hissed Adams, pulling him toward the door. "Don't let them see you. Get the license number. Call the SWAT team or whoever, a helicopter. I'll leave my phone on so you can trace it. 872, 414, 3414. Got it?"

"But you can't..." called the manager, Bradley, from behind them. But he trailed off, uncertain what a man could or couldn't do in this situation.

They were almost to the door.

"Promise me," said Adams, grim determination in his voice. "Promise me you'll find my wife and save her, no matter what happens to me."

"I can only promise we'll do our best," said the cop,

"Great," said Adams with disgust, and hurried down the stairs. He pushed through the door and out onto the street. He held his head high, a man going to the firing squad, the blue box clutched tightly in his left hand, his cell phone still gripped in his right.

As Adams crossed to the car, the cop looked through the window, holding his hand up behind him to warn everyone in the lobby to stay back. He watched as Adams slid the phone into his pocket and climbed into the back seat. The door closed and he disappeared behind tinted windows.

As the car pulled away, the cop rushed through the front doors of The Drake, just in time to see and memorize the license plate.

Then he turned toward his own car, pulling his phone from his pocket as he ran. A crowd of hotel guests had gathered at the door to watch. He reached his car in seconds, punching a number in his speed dial as he went. He wrenched the door open and jabbed the button that started the car, throwing it into drive before he had even slammed the door. Pulling into traffic one-handed, he looked up the street just in time to see the black town car turn right on to North Lake Shore Drive and disappear into the fading afternoon light. He gunned the engine in pursuit.

# 2

Adams sat in the back seat of the black town car and let out a long, satisfied sigh. In the front seat the driver turned to look at him. She had Japanese features and short black hair trimmed to her jawline. Her dark eyes flashed with mirth.

"By the grin on your face," she said, "I'm guessing it went well."

He waved the blue box in his hand.

"Keep your eyes on the road, this would be a bad time to get in an accident."

She turned forward but looked up into her rearview mirror.

"Are the police in hot pursuit?" she asked coyly.

Adams looked over his shoulder. "*Si*," he said. "Here he comes, fast and furiously. Oh, wait, he seems to have taken a wrong turn on to Division. Oh well. Who will save us now?"

He couldn't keep the smile off his face; the adrenaline was still coursing through his body. The feeling never got old.

"How did Danny do?" his wife asked from the front.

"Excellent," exclaimed Adams. "Really top notch. We owe the man a bonus."

"Do we, now?" she asked.

"Yes, Abby. No need to be greedy." He shook the box.

"You make it sound like we are going to keep all those diamonds for ourselves. Have you forgotten our client?"

Adams exhaled. "Of course not. But we should still celebrate. Dinner?"

"That sounds perfect. Raisu?"

"Okay," said the man, reaching up and pulling the blond wig off his head. Underneath his hair was dark and lustrous. He gingerly peeled the goatee off as well. "But let's stop at home first, I really need a quick shower."

"Then home it is. Would you like to go through the park?"

"Yes, my love, you know I love to go through the park."

***

From the small balcony of their tenth-floor condo, Mr. and Mrs. Adams looked out over the lights of the park below and Montrose Beach beyond that, and then out across Lake Michigan. It was dark but for a fragrant candle on a small table between their chairs.

Each of them had a spoon and a pint of Jeni's ice cream that they had picked up on their way home from the sushi restaurant. Salted Honey Pie for her and Strawberry Buttermilk for him.

It had been a busy few hours. Ditching the car, destroying their SIM cards and replacing them with new ones. The trip across town to Shelby Furniture, where they left the blue box, and the diamonds in it, with a man named Eldon Shelby. Then, finally, dinner.

Now, they stared out at the horizon, slowly spooning the delicious ice cream into their mouths. The woman groaned with satisfaction.

"My god, Love. Are you sure you don't want some of this?"

"I'm good with strawberry. Really good."

Abby rested her spoon in the near-empty container. "I think I'm done."

"No, you can do it. Perseverance, that's what I always say."

She looked over at his candlelit profile. "Someday, my love, there is going to be a best actor award for criminals, and you are sure to get it."

"Gracias. What do you think Bradley will do when the Ackerlys return to the hotel to find their diamonds gone?"

"Polish his resumé, I guess. Does it matter?"

"No, of course not. I just sometimes find myself thinking of the collateral damage." He frowned, still staring straight out over the lake, watching the lights of a slow-moving ship.

"That way madness lies."

"You're right," he shrugged, spooning the last of his ice cream into his mouth. "We're doing the right thing. This next one's going to be even better. Best yet."

"Oh god, not the next one yet. Wait a day, would you, before you start obsessing over the next one?"

"Sorry."

They turned to look at each other, and he admired her eyes reflecting in the candlelight, the smile lines at their corners, the few shining strands of gray in her hair, though she was only 38 years old. She picked the carton back up and took another bite of ice cream.

"You know what I'm thinking about?" she said in a low, throaty voice.

"Sex?"

"Yes," she said, winking. "That Eldon Shelby is so yummy I could eat him up, that dark hair and those sexy gray temples. His little brother, too."

"Oh, Christ," the man swore.

She chortled. "Maybe both Shelbys for dessert, if I weren't already so full of sushi."

Her husband lurched to his feet, grasping the railing.

"Oh, come on, Love," she set her container down. "It's just a joke."

"It's not funny."

"We're celebrating. We're supposed to be happy. You're so busy thinking about the next job you're only half here. I was just trying to get your attention. You know I'm just kidding."

He turned and walked through the sliding door and into the dark living room.

"I'm going for a run," he said woodenly over his shoulder.

"Damn it," she hissed under her breath, slapping the ice cream container off the table in frustration. The spoon bounced off the decking and through the railing, clattering on the pavement below a few seconds later.

\*\*\*

The next morning Abby stood in front of the bathroom mirror, which ran the full length of the two-sink marble countertop. She finished washing off yesterday's makeup, which she'd been too exhausted to do last night. She stared at the pink scar that ran from her forehead across her right eye and down her right cheek to her jaw. Her eyes continued down, past her small breasts to her bare stomach, and she ran a hand slowly across it. Finally, she reached for her makeup, then looked back at her face in the mirror.

Fuck it, she thought, she probably wasn't leaving the condo today. Wear the scar like a flag.

Walking back into the bedroom, she pulled her green bathrobe from the bedpost and slipped it on, tying the sash firmly.

The state of the sheets told her that John had come in and slept at some point, but she didn't remember it, and he was already up and gone when she awoke. So much for a night of celebration. She wasn't sure what it was that made her tease him when she shouldn't, but she couldn't

15

stand his progressive seriousness. It seemed each job just made him more and more dour, despite the fact that they had redirected so much money over the last five years. They were stunningly successful at what they did.

She walked into the main room of the condo, which was high-ceilinged and airy, with windows the length of one wall and an open-plan kitchen. On the long dining table was an immense house of playing cards. It covered most of the table and was at least three feet high. Red and blue patterned cards alternated precisely. He must have used at least thirty decks, she marveled, maybe more. Everyone has their own coping mechanisms; John had several.

She scanned the couch and glanced out through the sliding door to the deck. No John. She quietly opened the door and peered into the second bedroom. Their adopted teenage daughter didn't live with them anymore, but they kept the room ready for her in case she needed a place to stay. They had taken her in when they caught her trying to hustle them with a classic Morgan Inversion scheme. John always said it was the best one he'd ever seen—for a twelve-year-old. She'd been with them for five years until she decided she wanted to live on her own. She had an independent streak a mile wide. The room was empty, the bed unslept in. No John. Back in the main room, Abby made her way slowly around the table, careful not to cause any atmospheric disturbance. If he came home and found the house collapsed, he'd think she did it out of spite.

She felt the cool tile on her bare feet as she passed from the living area into the kitchen, where the red light of the coffeemaker glowed. She smiled, feeling a bit better. He had made the coffee before he left, and he didn't drink coffee.

***

Adams stood on the beach in the morning light, progressing from standing pose to tree pose, so slowly he barely seemed to move. Runners and dog walkers passed by, some glancing at him, some ignoring him completely. He had a bad back, from a horrific fall long ago, but years of daily yoga had all but eliminated the pain.

It was early fall, still the end of summer, really, and the sun felt good.

He took deep, calming breaths, still furious with himself for being an ass last night. He tried to remove all thoughts from his mind and bring his focus back to his breathing.

Nothing but the breath.

And the next one. And the next.

He sighed and lowered his bare foot to the sand. Her face swam before him, and he would not banish it in the name of inner peace.

Why was he so angry all the time? Why did it seem like there was never enough time? They had all the time in the world. They owed nothing to nobody. He thought back to his difficult life as a destitute teenager in this tough city, and before that to his life in another world. Every day had been a struggle. With Abby, each day should feel like a vacation. But more and more, it didn't, and he knew it wasn't her fault.

He sat down on the beach in his black cotton pants and black T-shirt. His dark hair was just long enough to feel the breeze blowing through it. He closed his eyes. He tried again to empty his mind, but he knew it was no good, so he shifted his focus to the one thing he knew would keep his brain occupied.

The next job.

On the dark screen of his imagination, he set up the chess pieces and worked his way through the puzzle, one step at a time. Playing it out again and again until he could see the bright, beautiful solution that had been there all the time, just waiting for him to find it.

# 3

Abby Adams wore her natural hair, her face made up with foundation and lipstick. Dark glasses covered her eyes as she sat in the sunny window seat of the coffee shop. The sour mood of the morning was dissipating. After all, the job at The Drake had gone off without a hitch, moving them one step closer to their goals. Not that this was a surprise. All of their jobs tended to go off without a hitch. John would have the next job completely mapped out by the time she got home and he'd be as excited as a kid at Christmas, his surliness forgotten.

She had never cheated on him, and he knew that. She didn't know why the joke about Eldon and Nick Shelby had upset him so. Yes, he had trust issues, deep-seated from childhood and a life on the street, but if there were two people in the world he could trust, it was Eldon and herself. Maybe that was it: The thought of the two people closest to him betraying him at the same time.

She sipped her coffee. It was hard sometimes, in a business where lying and misdirection were your stock-in-trade, to not assume everyone else had a side hustle going as well.

She saw Danny pass by the window and a moment later he entered the shop and sat across from her.

"Just you today?" he asked with a smile.

"Just me, if that's okay," Abby said, removing her sunglasses and setting them on the little cafe table.

"'Course it's okay. I like John and all, but really, he's a bore."

"Exactly."

"And what a whiner! You should have heard him the other day: 'Who are you? What have you done with my wife?' Blah blah blah."

Danny was funny, and a good guy. She was going to miss him.

"Look Danny, I'm sorry to drag you down here in the middle of the day, but I just wanted to make the offer one last time. Full partner. We need more people, and we trust you."

Danny ran his palm over his close-cropped hair.

"I thought a lot about it. I really did. But I can't do it anymore. The risk is too great. I want to get married, maybe have a kid. Write a novel."

"A novel?" She raised her eyebrows.

"Sure, why not?"

"I thought you had a business degree."

"So? Wallace Stevens was an insurance salesman."

She stared at him blankly.

"He was a poet. Never mind. Besides, I thought you were working on an exit strategy."

Abby snorted. "I'm working on one, and John acts like he is. Each job gets bigger than the last, but I think we could hit Fort Knox and it still wouldn't be enough for him." She leaned a bit closer and lowered her voice. "This next one is really a step up, it could be the home run we've been waiting for, but we need a bigger crew. Are you sure you aren't interested?"

Danny leaned away from her, a sad smile on his face.

"Look, Abby. I love you guys, but I gotta move on. It's not about the money for me, I've put enough away for a decade. I'm enrolled at The University of Chicago for graduate courses starting in January. Something I should have done years ago." He stood up and looked down at her. "If you're in a pinch over the next few weeks, like that thing with the guy a few weeks ago, you call me, and I'll help any way I can. But I don't want to be part of the plan, or part of the crew. Nothing big like The Drake again."

She took another sip of her coffee as she watched his broad back head for the door. Shit. There weren't many as dependable and talented as Danny. They would have to broaden their search.

***

Madeleine Levesque was a lieutenant with the Chicago police. As such, she expected a bit more respect than she was getting at the moment from this rich bitch. Spoiled, suburban, Pilates-loving, Mercedes-driving, rich bitch. That's what she was thinking to herself as she leaned back against the massive granite-topped island counter in Marion Menard's kitchen.

She checked out Menard's leotard-sheathed body as the woman reached up into a cabinet to pull down a water glass. One glass; she hadn't even bothered to offer Levesque any refreshment.

The woman wasn't all that hot, Levesque decided. Sure, for forty years old, she supposed she was in good shape. Levesque looked down at her own thirty-four-year-old body, arms crossed over her chest. Menard would probably gas out if she tried the Chicago PD physical training course, a course whose women's record time was held by Levesque herself. For the last three years, in fact. Menard had been talking, but Levesque hadn't been listening. She was still fuming about being forced to come all the way out here for what could have been handled in five minutes on the phone. But her boss had insisted. Apparently, the Menards knew a lot of the right people. Typical.

The rich couple had experienced a home invasion earlier in the summer while they were away on vacation.

Lots of expensive trinkets were taken, but not much else. A serious attempt on the house safe, but it was a serious safe and it rebuffed all attempts. Levesque and her team had dusted for prints, reviewed the in-house surveillance system (better than most banks she'd been in), and done a thorough door-to-door. Nothing.

"Nothing!" the woman was saying when Levesque tuned back in. "As far as I can tell, you've accomplished absolutely nothing."

"Now wait a minute, Ms. Menard. I've logged a lot of hours on this case. Just because we haven't found any leads doesn't mean we haven't been working every angle. We have."

Marion Menard frowned at her as she set the glass of water on the counter, opened a drawer, and took out a packet of protein powder.

"Are you sure about that?" She opened the packet and emptied it into her glass, grabbing a spoon from the drawer.

Levesque raised an eyebrow, her arms still clenched across her chest. Now this woman was going to tell her how to do her job?

"Meaning what, exactly?" she asked, keeping her voice calm.

"Well, don't you have contacts in the criminal world? Confidential informants, etc? Surely somebody knows who robbed us." Her spoon made a clink-clink-clinking sound against the side of the glass as the water turned pink.

"That's mostly TV and the movies," Levesque said, trying to keep the derision out of her voice. She was going to have a word with the chief when she got back downtown. Not that it would do shit-all.

"That's not what I heard," Menard was saying. "I heard about this husband and wife team that robs rich people

22

and bad guys. You know, like Robin Hood."

Levesque's jaw clenched so hard it seemed her teeth would crumble. She uncrossed her arms and turned so that she was facing Menard square on, directly across the island counter. She leaned forward and gripped the granite counter top, her fingers turning white from the strain.

"Tell me what you know about these people," she growled.

Marion blanched and took a step back.

"Well, nothing really..."

"Did you meet with them?"

"Well, I..."

"This is serious, Ms. Menard. These are wanted criminals, for many, many crimes. Did you hire them?"

"Well, it didn't seem like I was getting any help from the poli—"

Levesque released her grip on the counter and slapped her palm down on the counter top.

"They are not good people, Ms. Menard. I've been chasing them for some time. What you're hearing is an urban myth. There are no honorable thieves. How do you know they weren't the ones who robbed you in the first place?"

"They only rob bad people, and the rich," Marion insisted. "That's what my friend told me."

Levesque just raised her eyebrows again and glanced around the spacious kitchen. Marion followed her gaze.

"What? Us? We aren't rich. Well, not rich rich, if you know what I mean. Not like Kenilworth rich."

Levesque's eyebrows did not lower.

"They took my first husband's wedding ring!" Marion Menard exclaimed, heat rising in her face. "I'm a widower, you know. He was a saint. If I'd been home when it happened, I'd have opened the safe and given them anything in exchange for that ring."

"I understand—"

"I don't think you do, or you would have found my ring by now!"

Levesque held up both hands in surrender, her training kicking in, bringing down her temper.

"Ms. Menard, please. Let's take a step back. I apologize if I've upset you. You questioned my professionalism and I took it badly. I shouldn't have done that. You don't know me, and I can understand how the loss of something dear to you would upset you."

She watched as Menard's shoulders dropped slightly, and then she continued.

"These people you've hired, they aren't heroes, and they aren't your friends or your champions. They are criminals and they are responsible for a lot of the robberies in this city."

Marion looked suddenly scared. "But, but they aren't violent, I mean, they aren't responsible for all the shooting in the city, or the drugs."

"We don't know that," said Levesque, which was actually a lie. She was pretty sure the couple restricted their crimes to grand theft, but Menard didn't need to know that. "We need to find them, and if we find them, then hopefully we can get your ring and your other valuables back. How do they contact you?"

"I have a phone number," she offered.

"Could I have it, please?"

Menard looked uncertain. Whatever had been said, they had really convinced her that they could get her beloved husband's ring back. Levesque wondered what Marion's current husband thought about her attachment to the old keepsake. Oh well, not her problem. She'd been after these mysterious thieves for a couple of years, and so far, all she had were whispers and suggestions. This

24

could be a big break.

"Marion?"

"It's just..."

"You paid them already, didn't you?"

"Well yes, they wanted half the money up front."

Levesque looked down and shook her head slowly.

"Okay. I get it, I was stupid. I'll go get their number. They gave me a business card."

She strode purposely out of the kitchen and down a long hallway, her sneakers squeaking on the marble floor.

Levesque was watching her go, thinking this could be her big break, when her phone rang.

"Levesque... No, I'm way out in Snobville on this Menard thing.... What?... At the Drake?... Why are we just finding about it now?... What off-duty officer?... Oh Christ, okay. I'll be there as soon as I can. What have you got for footage?"

Levesque sighed and pinched the bridge of her nose.

"Of course the cameras malfunctioned. Of course.... No, hang tight. I'll finish up here and meet you there in twenty."

She hung up the phone, barely refraining from smashing it on the expensive granite countertop.

# 4

Adams smashed the wooden chair over the old woman's head, sending her crashing to the ground. Her gun skittered across the hardwood floor and into a corner.

Jesus Christ, this evening wasn't going quite as he had planned. Hand-to-hand combat with senior citizens. Only half an hour ago, it had been a friendly game of blackjack.

\*\*\*

Adams gathered the cards and shuffled them with practiced ease. Cards were one of his talismans. He loved the feel of them in his hands, loved the sound of them as they were shuffled together, the whisper of them as they slid in a slow spin across the table, one at a time, coming to rest perfectly in front of each person.

There were five of them, but the dim room held three other tables, each with four or five people at them. There was also a bar, with the usual mirror and shelves of bottles behind it. The standard surly bartender leaned on his elbows while looking at his phone. He was a big bruiser, but nothing compared to the two hulks working the door, dressed in matching beige suits with black ties and dark sunglasses. Beige wasn't the best look on them, especially in fall. Adams felt at home in his lightweight black suit over a crisp white Oxford, no tie.

He looked for the sky to see if it was dawn yet, but there were no windows in the room. Besides the bathroom, there was only one door and it led back into the main room of the club. This room was for high-stakes players only. Through the door he heard the sound of a rack of balls being broken on one of the many billiard tables. It was late, but apparently they weren't the only ones left in the building.

He looked at his two cards quickly, then glanced around the table at his opponents. Straight across from him sat an older woman, maybe sixty, and a kid who seemed to be in high school, though as Adams got older it seemed harder and harder to tell. The guy wore a Northwestern T-shirt and had unruly brown curls and a few days of scruff. Or maybe a few weeks, if he was a teenager. Not that it mattered; the kid played a good game. A little wooden, a little math-heavy, but a good game.

On either side of Adams as he dealt sat two hard-looking guys. The one on his right was tall and slim, but he had a nasty set to his face and an ugly scar on his neck. John thought instantly of Abby but brought his focus quickly back to the game.

"Hit me," said the man on his left, and Adams dealt him a nine.

"Shit," the guy said, rubbing one hand over his shaved head and tossing his cards in with the other. "Not even gonna bother to fake it with this one." He grunted in disgust. He was in his mid-thirties but had seen some wear and tear. He had a curly black beard and oversized arm muscles. A tattoo of a snake slithered up from the collar of his navy-blue Oxford shirt. He had the sleeves rolled up and a big gold watch glistened on his left wrist.

Adams snuck a look at it. Four AM. Jesus, he was never going to get out of here.

"Check," said the woman, and Adams revised his estimate upward. She was maybe seventy, with heavy-framed red plastic glasses that hung from a beaded chain around her neck. Each time she got a card, she lifted the glasses to her face without quite putting them on, read the card, and then let the glasses drop back down to her chest. She wore a blue knit button-down sweater to defend her from the arctic air conditioning that was chugging in through a unit mounted high on the wall. It was a warm night outside for September, and the AC provided some ventilation in the windowless room.

The kid fidgeted. "Hit me," he said finally, so Adams gave him a three. A look of agony crossed the kid's face. His math was telling him to take another card, but nobody likes to take a hit with a fifteen. Adams felt bad, momentarily, for messing with him.

"Again?"

"Wait a minute," the kid snapped. Then finally, "I'll hold."

It didn't matter. The tall man had a king showing and Adams knew there was an ace underneath.

"Fifty," the guy said with a grin, tossing some chips into the middle.

Adams looked the man square in the eye with a searching look. The tall man stared back placidly. After another five seconds Adams broke his gaze away, shook his head, and smiled a goofy smile. "I'm going to be sorry I did this, but I'm in." He added his chips to the pile and looked to the old woman. "Ma'am?"

"Ma'am your goddam self," she said, and threw her cards down, folding.

Adams turned to the tall man, who nodded once.

"I'm good," he said.

"Okay then," said Adams, revealing his ten and his jack. "Twenty."

The tall man just grinned and revealed his ace.

"Aw, damn," said Adams. "I really didn't think you had it."

"I had it." He pulled the chips toward him.

The man with the beard and the watch noticed that two of the other tables were wrapping it up. He stretched and looked around. "Call it a night?"

"I got class," said the kid, getting up.

"That's not what I heard," said the old woman and chortled at her own joke. The kid left without looking back. For a moment the sounds of people playing pool were louder as half the room made its way out the door. Adams could hear bad eighties hair metal playing on the sound system out there and shuddered.

"I wouldn't mind a chance to win some of my money back," he said, looking at the tall man with the scar.

"Yeah, me too," said the bearded man, "but I need a drink first." He stood and looked around the table. "Can I get anyone something?"

"PBR," said the old woman without hesitation.

"Nothing for me," said the tall man.

"Club soda would be great," said Adams. "Thanks."

"Right, I'll be back in a second. You can take my deal."

The old woman gathered up the cards and shuffled while they waited for the drinks.

The bearded man returned carrying the can of beer, the club soda, and a green Heineken bottle. He set them on the table.

"Great," said Adams, nodding toward the door, "now I've got 'Living on a Prayer' stuck in my head."

"Not a bad song," said the bearded man with a shrug.

Adams laughed. "It always reminds me of my friend Danny O'Brian. We would go to concerts at Wrigley Field and once we nearly got arrested with some girls out by the center-field wall."

"Wait a minute," the bearded man interrupted, "I heard this story. Redheaded guy?"

"Yeah, hard to have a name like Danny O'Brian and not have red hair. You know him?"

29

"I met him in a bar on Roscoe last week, we were talking about best concerts and he was telling me about he and his friend Adams getting blow jobs up against the ivy in outfield —"

"Oh, for Christ's sake," growled the old woman and began dealing the cards.

Adams blushed and checked his cards, he had a queen and a seven.

"You Adams, then?" the bearded man asked.

"Yeah," he answered, still looking embarrassed. "That was a long time ago, though. Happily married now."

"He told me all about you."

"Nothing bad, I hope?" Adams smiled.

"No, he said you were..." His voice trailed off as a shadow crossed his face.

"What?"

"Nothing," said the man, recovering. "Just said you were a good guy. A holy terror. Fold." He threw his hand down on the table.

***

The game continued for another twenty minutes, during which Adams repeatedly caught the bearded man looking at him, then looking at the tall man and his ever-growing pile of chips.

"I think we should raise the stakes," said the tall man.

"I don't know," said Adams, "it's getting late."

"I thought you wanted to win your money back?" he said, barely containing his contempt.

"Oh, ah. Well, okay. I guess one more wouldn't hurt."

The bearded man pushed his chair back. "I think I'll sit this one out," he said. "Gotta use the bathroom."

"Lizzie?" The tall man asked, looking at the old woman.

"I'm in," she growled, and passed him the cards.

In Vegas, they swap out decks of cards every two to four hours. In mafia-connected backrooms of Chicago sports bars, they aren't as picky. Adams counted on that, and on the fact that your average card sharp couldn't tell how many cards were in a deck just by shuffling them.

He was dealt a nine face up, a six underneath. That would work just fine. In the right sleeve of his black sport coat he had sequestered a three of hearts and a four of diamonds, removed from the deck surreptitiously the third time he had been the dealer. In the left sleeve he had the two of hearts and tucked into the top of his black pants was the five of clubs, all acquired the same way, slowly, over the course of the evening. He would have liked an ace, but any decent player would notice an ace missing after a few hands.

And make no mistake, the tall man was a good player. Adams had noticed him dealing off the bottom with the grace and misdirection of a pro. No one who wasn't looking for it intently would ever have spotted it.

Lizzie had a jack showing, and the tall man had a nine.

The tall man looked at Adams, who tossed a fifty-dollar chip into the pot. Lizzie matched it, but the tall man raised five hundred.

"Oh, come on, now," grimaced Adams.

"You agreed to raise the stakes," said the tall man evenly.

Lizzie tossed in the additional chips. Adams sighed and did the same.

"Hit me," he said.

The tall man placed a nine face up on Adams hand, right next to the nine that was already there. Adams turned and looked at the tall man, who blithely raised an eyebrow at him. He reached forward and lifted his hand, looking at the card underneath as the tall man turned toward Lizzie expectantly.

"I'll stay," said the old woman.

"I'll stay as well," said the tall man and set down the deck, assuming Adams, with eighteen showing and a card underneath, would also be staying.

"Mr. Adams, are you bidding?" he asked.

Adams kept a stony look on his face. "No, thank you."

"Folding?"

"No," he sighed. "I'll pass."

"Pass," said Lizzie as well.

The tall man pushed a large tower of chips into the middle. "Five thousand," he grinned.

"Asshole," said Lizzie, tossing her cards down.

"Sorry," said the tall man. "When you have the cards, you've got to bid big. And nobody plays this game like I do."

Adams barked out a laugh.

"You think it's funny?"

"I do," said Adams calmly, pushing his own pile of chips into the middle. "Your five, and another five."

The man had an incredulous look on his face, but it settled into a knowing smile. He looked down at the table in front of him. "You think I don't have enough cash? You think you can strong arm me out?" He raised his right hand and snapped his fingers. At the table across the room, where four men still played, quiet fell immediately. One of the men stood, gathered his chips, and brought them across the room, placing them in a neat stack in front of the tall man.

Adams looked startled but kept his calm. "You brought friends, Brock?"

The tall man raised his eyebrows again. "You know my name? Interesting, and yes, I brought some friends along for a pleasant night out. Bachelor party." He pushed the pile of chips into the middle of the table. "I call," he said, and flipped his card over to reveal an ace, which he placed next to his nine. "Twenty."

Adams kept his eyes locked on Brock as he reached forward and flipped his facedown card. What had once been a six of hearts was now a three of hearts.

"Twenty-one."

Brock exploded.

He jumped up and back, sending his wooden chair over backwards, pulling a pistol from the back of his belt. Adams stood as well, grabbing his chair with his right hand as he did, to keep it from falling over and to give him something to grip, since he didn't have a gun. He heard the scraping of chairs from the other table as Brock's men also sprang to attention. Out of the corner of his eye he saw one of the large men guarding the door step forward, both hands up in a calming gesture.

"Hey now," the guard said, while the other guard locked the door, at the same time reaching up to swing down a wooden brace that fit across the door, as if securing a medieval castle.

"You fucking cheat!" growled Brock.

"Now, why do you say that?" asked Adams, attempting to stay calm.

"No way you had a fucking three under there!"

"Why, because you know what you dealt me?"

"Of course not," he said quickly, but his face twitched for just an instant, enough to cause Lizzie to stand. From somewhere in her handbag she produced a good-sized revolver, which she pointed at the tall man.

"Really, Brock? You have the balls to cheat when I'm at the table?" Her voice sounded more disappointed than angry.

"Everyone relax," said the big guard, stepping toward the center of the room. "Friendly cards, here. Just friendly cards."

33

Lizzie snorted and just then the bathroom door banged open as the bearded man came out into the room. All heads turned toward him, and Adams took that moment to swing his chair up and around at Brock, who managed to lean back just in time. The chair continued its arc and smashed into Lizzie, sending her down to the ground and her gun skittering off across the hardwood floor and into a corner.

"Jesus Christ!" said the bearded man, as the four men at the other table started across the room toward Adams and Brock. They were met in the middle by the two guards, both of whom were at least six inches taller than any of Brock's guys. Whether that would matter in a gun fight remained to be seen. One of Brock's men reached into his jacket but was tackled to the ground before he could pull out whatever was in there. Adams and Brock faced each other, Brock's gun pointing directly at Adams's chest.

"I don't know what you think I did," Adams said calmly, "but it hardly matters. You were clearly stacking the deck."

Brock didn't move.

"You obviously made a mistake on that hand. Must have given me the—"

He was interrupted by a gunshot, and froze, waiting for a pain that never came.

Another gunshot followed and the wooden floor splintered by Adams's foot. A man yelled and furniture was broken, then silence fell again. Adams wanted to turn and look but didn't dare take his eyes off Brock.

"Listen, Brock," Adams tried again, staring at the tall man.

Brock stared back but then his eyes moved suddenly up and to the right, tracking something, a bottle, which sailed directly at his head. He brought his arm up, a second too late, which was all the opening Adams needed to lunge forward, grabbing Brock's wrist with both hands and turning the gun down and away while burying his shoulder in Brock's stomach, glass raining down on him as the empty beer bottle smashed off Brock's skull.

They went down in a heap, and when Brock did not immediately move, Adams twisted harder on his wrist, grabbing the gun away. Moving quickly, Adams rolled over Brock and then rolled once more until he came up to a sitting position at the far end of the room, back against the wall, gun braced out in front of him.

"Freeze," he barked, his voice loud and deep, his hand steady as he took in the scene. Everyone who could put their hands up, did.

Brock lay in front of him, moaning and clutching his head. Blood oozed between his long bony fingers. The old woman lay unconscious where Adams had struck her with the chair. At least he hoped she was just unconscious. Killing the elderly was not part of his plan.

All the chairs and tables were turned over; broken glass was everywhere. The bartender was nowhere to be seen, but at the end of the bar nearest the bathroom stood the bearded man, his hands held up in front of him. On the floor in the center of the room most of Brock's team lay in a heap. Adams saw a lot of blood, but mostly on faces, not the kind of pooling on the floor that he had come to associate with fatal gunshots. He spotted a switchblade lying alone on the floor near the door, blood on the glinting blade. There was moaning, and moving, but no one seemed able or willing to do anything rash.

Just behind them, one of the big doormen had gripped the edge of the bar with both hands and was slowly pulling himself to his feet. When he finally made it, he gave a great exhale and then raised his arms from his sides, turned slowly around until he was facing Adams, and leaned back against the bar. He had a big split over one cheekbone, blood oozing down the side of his face. The pointer and middle finger of his right hand were broken at an angle that must have been extremely painful. His raised hands pulled his suit jacket open wide enough for Adams to see that he didn't have a gun.

His partner was seated on the floor, slumped against the door to the main room, his head down. Adams wondered if he was faking, but just then someone pounded hard on the outer door. The man didn't rouse at all.

Adams stood and turned his attention to the bearded man. "Did you throw that bottle?"

The man nodded.

"Thanks. What's your name?"

The man gave a little half-grin. "Rather not say at the moment," he said, glancing at the big man leaning against the other end of the bar.

Adams nodded. "I can understand that. Where's the bartender?"

The bearded man gestured behind the bar.

"Mind if I step back there and take a look?"

Adams nodded. The man lowered his hands and moved behind the bar. He knelt out of sight. A moment later he stood back up with a shotgun in his hand.

Adams tensed, but the man set the weapon on the top of the bar and stepped away from it.

"Loaded?" Adams asked.

The man looked back at the shotgun.

"Doesn't appear to be."

"Check, please," Adams said. "He dead?"

"No, but he's out."

Adams turned to the guard.

"What's your name?"

"Parker," said the man. He was still breathing heavily,

holding a cloth napkin to the side of his face to staunch the blood.

"Your partner okay?"

"Dunno."

"Check, please."

The big man staggered over to his partner, leaned down and tipped his head back, eliciting a moan.

"He's fine," said Parker and let go of his head.

Adams raised his eyebrow. The guy didn't look fine. There was more pounding from the other side of the barred door.

Adams gestured toward the door. "What's the protocol?"

"Why should I tell you?" Parker replied, but his voice was calm.

Adams took a step forward, purposely placing his right foot onto the fingers of Brock's outstretched left hand. There was a snap and a groan from the floor.

"Because Brock is a piece of shit. Because I came here, unarmed, to play cards and he tried to rip me off and then he tried to kill me. I didn't start this, and I don't see why it should end with me in jail."

The guard pulled the napkin away from his face, appraised the blood there, and then pushed it to his face again. He glanced at the door.

"Serious trouble breaks out, 'specially gun trouble, our job is to secure the door until the police arrive. Protect the regular customers, figure no one back here is innocent."

"Tough on you," said Adams.

He shrugged. "Yeah, well, the pay is good."

"So how do we get out?" asked the bearded man.

"You don't," said Parker. "Cops'll be here any minute. Till then, I make sure it stays shut."

The bearded man scoffed at this bravado, but Adams

just nodded. He turned to his new compatriot.

"What about the bathroom?"

"No chance," said the bearded man. "Just one window, only about eight inches high, two feet wide, cranks open. Walls are cinder block."

Adams looked at him with surprise.

"What?" the man grinned. "I like to know where my exits are."

In the distance, they heard the first siren.

Adams kept the gun up, just in case, his eyes making rounds of the bodies in the room, checking for unexpected movement. One of Brock's men had made it into a sitting position, both hands clutching broken ribs.

"Okay," said Adams, looking back at Parker as the siren grew closer. "I've got to get out of here so that you can get these people some medical help." He took his foot off Brock's fingers and backed slowly toward the cinder block wall behind him, still holding the gun in his right hand. With his left he beckoned the bearded man to his side.

"You ever been in here before?" he asked.

"First time," the man shrugged. "Looking to meet the right people."

"Brock is not the right people."

"Know that now, don't I?"

"Take a cloth from behind the bar and clean our table, the bathroom, the shotgun, everything you touched."

"But how are we going to get out of here?"

"Just do it, we've got two minutes if we're lucky."

The bearded man ran to the bar, grabbed a wet cloth, and wiped down the shotgun. Then he headed into the bathroom.

Adams turned back to Parker and lifted his gun until the barrel pointed at the ceiling.

"Am I good to put this away?" he asked levelly.

Parker grimaced, or maybe smiled. It was hard for Adams to tell with the napkin and all the blood.

"Yeah, fine. Whatever. I gotta say I'm curious."

Adams put the gun in his waistband and then stepped along the wall until he reached the big, chugging air conditioner. Moving quickly—he didn't like to have his back to the room— he grabbed a chair and stood on it, grabbed either side of the unit and pulled hard.

It came away easily; it had likely never been properly installed, and since then someone had tampered with it. The unit crashed to the ground, pulling the cord from the wall as it fell.

The bearded man rushed back from the bathroom, looking around to see what had caused the noise. His gaze rested on the two-foot-square hole in the wall, and he barked with laughter.

"Thirty seconds," said Adams, and hoisted himself up and through the hole as his new friend rushed across the wreckage of the room to join him. The bearded man couldn't help but take a last look back at the room and give Parker a little wave.

"See you later, suckers!"

***

The bearded man dropped to the ground, his feet splashing in a puddle that was half water, half trash. He was glad he had his shitkickers on. He looked around to realize he was surrounded on all sides by cement and brick, the close walls of an air shaft. Adams was nowhere in sight.

"What th—?"

"Up here!" hissed a voice from above. He looked up to see Adams halfway up the wall, climbing an old metal ladder affixed to the side of the building. He moved fast for a guy in his forties.

A minute later they were on the roof and out of sight of anyone who might stick their head through the hole in the wall.

Adams leaned close. "Let's go, they'll be up here soon. There's no place else we could have gone."

They moved quickly across the rooftop until they came to the next building, which was a story taller than the one they were on, and snug up against it. Several windows looked out over the roof they stood on, but Adams headed instead for a ladder that would take them to the next roof. It leaned haphazardly against the brick wall, next to several buckets of grout and an old cooler. Empty beer cans lay scattered around.

Silently, they made their way up and across that roof to the next building, which was the same height. This continued across three more buildings until they finally reached an alley. The man was afraid Adams was going to try and jump across, but no, the mysterious card player peered down over the edge, moved ten feet to the right, and then climbed over the low brick retaining wall and onto a fire escape.

Moments later they stood breathing heavily under the cover of trees in a small park.

"Okay, okay. Now tell me, what the hell was that about?"

Adams kept his eyes on the quiet street. "Brock was cheating."

"Yeah, I got that part, man. I also got that you were letting him."

Adams brought his gaze back to the man, who was short, only about five foot seven, but probably close to two hundred pounds. Mostly muscle.

"What's your name?"

The bearded man hesitated, but only for a second.

"Jacob Kirk."

"I've heard of you," said Adams, his voice still quiet.

"Yeah?" said Kirk, surprised.

"Dunning area, protection, suspected larceny."

Kirk took a step back. "You a cop?"

"Do I look like a cop?"

Kirk snorted. "Everyone looks like a cop to me."

"I'm not a cop."

"O'Brian said you run some of the best jobs in the city."

"Exaggeration, but I do have my talents."

"I saw."

The two men hadn't broken eye contact. "Time to go," said Adams, looking up the street. They could hear the sound of police on the other end of the block, though there was no sign of them here yet. Still, best to be careful.

"Hang on," said Kirk, reaching for Adams's arm and then thinking better of it. "I'm not in Dunning. Not anymore. Been working out of Ravenswood the last four months."

Adams raised an eyebrow. "Moving up in the world?"

"World's getting tougher, I'm getting older." He shook his head wistfully. "I'm trying to move away from smash and grab to something a little more..."

"Elegant?"

"Lucrative," grinned Kirk. "Time to start planning for retirement."

Adams turned to go. "Well, thanks for the help."

"If you need help again..." Kirk said, trying to keep the eagerness out of his voice.

Adams turned back. "I think that would be a bad idea. You run ten, twelve men from what I hear?"

"Fifteen," said Kirk. He pulled his shoulders back, his chest puffing slightly.

"Can't see you wanting to follow my directions. Still..." Adams pulled his wallet from inside his dark suit coat and withdrew a business card, handed it to Kirk.

John Adams, it said. The Levelers Co., and below that a phone number.

"What do you level, then?" asked Kirk, but when he looked up Adams was twenty feet away, stepping into the passenger side of a black car that had rolled noiselessly up to the edge of the park.

# 5

"I'm so sorry, Miss..." she glanced down at the card in her hand but didn't have her reading glasses on and couldn't remember what the name on it had been.

"Okata."

"Okata. I'm sorry for all the trouble." The tall woman tilted her head sideways, the look on her face not quite as apologetic as her voice. Something didn't feel right to her, but she couldn't put her finger on it. She once again appraised the small Asian woman in front of her.

Heavy makeup, with dark red lipstick that seemed more sensual than someone from an alarm company should be wearing. Of course, she wasn't just some engineer or maintenance worker. According to her business card she was the Vice-President of New Business Development, whatever that meant.

And her hair. The woman was clearly of Asian descent, though her hair was a white blonde with streaks of black underneath. That combination always struck her as odd. It was unrealistic—jarringly so—which was fine for a young hipster, but this woman was an executive, somewhere in her thirties, if she had to guess.

Okata held up the small green circuit board again. One end was blackened and melted.

"No worry, Mrs. Hendricks, I—"

"Miss."

"—appreciate good security, and I had no appointment. As I mentioned, I was here in The Rookery Building for a meeting at Ringwald and Shepard when my device let me know that your alarm had tripped." Her heavy accent stumbled slightly on the name of the building. "So I called dispatch and hurried over. But I could have been anyone, you were right to be suspicious."

Hendricks stared at the melted piece of hardware. Twenty minutes ago, she had been at her desk in her office, door slightly ajar, working on the October personnel schedule when she heard raised voices in the lobby.

"I'm sorry, ma'am, but no one from our IT department even works in this building. It's all done remotely." Jenny had seemed flustered, so Hendricks stepped around her desk and strode into the lobby, where this blonde woman was talking rapidly and gesturing wildly with her right hand, which held an oversized Samsung device. The device was emitting a loud, rhythmic beeping sound.

It was the end of the day, Royal and James were both gone, and Eleanor Hendricks figured she was likely the ranking executive currently in the Grafton Corp office. Well, Lionel was still here, but he was in a meeting.

As Director of Human Resources, she felt more than a little out of her element as she listened to the woman, Okata, tell her about the Hoppleton Security Coupler, or whatever it was she was yammering on about as they walked briskly through the office toward the server room at the back. Hendricks was supposed to be leading the way, but Okata moved so quickly she had to hustle to keep up.

It was somewhat reassuring that Okata seemed to know exactly where she was going, straight to the unmarked door, where she stopped and waited while Hendricks applied her thumb to a fingerprint scanner set next to the door. They passed through to a long hallway and, at the end, a door to the temperature-controlled server room. The woman followed her in and strode straight to one particular bank of computers.

Okata turned to her.

"Do you have any needle-nose pliers? No? Of course not, what am I thinking, you're the president of the company."

"Just Director of Human Resources," Hendricks corrected her, instantly picturing the Grafton brothers in her mind.

"Oh, I just thought by the way you took charge of the situation..."

"We pride ourselves on preparedness."

"Sounds like a great slogan."

"It is."

"Excuse me?" Okata was only half listening. She set her phone, still beeping, and her handbag on a nearby desk and started rifling through the drawers.

"It is our slogan. Grafton Corp. We pride ourselves on preparedness."

"Okay." Okata straightened up, a long screwdriver with a yellow handle in her hand. "I know what you mean. Look at me." She set the screwdriver on the desk, unbuttoned her suit coat, removed it, and folded it neatly. "I've been the head of my division for three years, haven't done any field work in twice that time." She set the coat on the desk and picked up the screwdriver again. It looked incongruous, huge in her small hand, and a stark contrast to the crisp white shirt and dark blue pinstripe pants she wore. "But when an A4 alarm goes off for one of our best customers, and I'm in the building, well..."

"Well?" repeated Hendricks, not sure where this was heading.

"Well, I do this," said Okata and, suddenly lying on the floor on her back, she wiggled her shoulders and pushed with her feet until her entire upper body disappeared through the fourteen-inch gap between the bottom of the server rack and the floor.

"Oh dear, Miss Okata, I don't think you should be doing that."

"It's fine," came the muffled voice. "I was in the tech department for five years." She grunted, and said something under her breath in Japanese, or Chinese, Hendricks wasn't sure. "Their manuals were terrible, so I rewrote them all. Turned out I had a knack for translating technical ideas into plain English, so they put me on new customer training." The woman's phone, still sitting on the desk, suddenly stopped beeping. "That led to new customer acquisition. I landed a string of big-time clients, including Illcom and Archer Daniels Midland, and suddenly presto," she wiggled out from under the server rack, "I'm an executive."

She struggled to her feet, a smile on her face. "Look."

In her hand she held a blackened, melted piece of circuit board.

"Oh my gosh," said Hendricks.

"It's okay," said Okata. She handed the damaged piece to Hendricks and set the screwdriver on the desk. She picked up her Samsung and typed rapidly. "I've canceled the call; you should be all set."

"But don't you need to put in a new one?"

Okata laughed. "No, I've bypassed it, and back at headquarters they are already uploading the security files to one of the other servers." She turned her device toward Hendricks, who could see a little red bar progressing across the screen with the word "loading" flashing underneath it. Okata put on her jacket, picked up her bag, and headed for the door. Hendricks followed. It was hard not to let this woman take the lead. As they walked through the cubicles and back toward the lobby, she saw herself briefly in her mind, too shy to be like this spitfire, still at her little desk year after year as one of the male executives rushed off to meet a client at The Capital Grille

46

or The Palm. People like Lionel Banke.

No sooner did she think his name than the door to his office, on the other side of the large sea of cubicles, opened and Banke walked out with a young woman in tow. Banke was a former running back for the Chicago Bears. He was well over six feet tall, African American, with impossibly broad shoulders and a gleaming bald head. When he played in the '90s, the crowd would chant, "Take it to the Banke!" over and over until he was given the ball. Then they would cheer wildly. When the Grafton brothers found out Banke had a degree in economics, they jumped at the chance to have him on their "team," doing commercials and wooing clients.

Today, Hendricks thought he looked unhappy, though handsome as ever. He had a grim look on his face as he headed toward the back stairs, not glancing at the girl who followed behind him. Girl? Woman? She was perhaps a college student, tall with coffee-colored skin and clothes that looked both expensive and haphazard at the same time. Her hair was long and straightened, and she carried a huge tote bag over her shoulder.

She seemed too young to be a girlfriend, even for Banke, who had a reputation with the ladies. Not that Hendricks, at fifty-five, had ever had a chance to find out about those rumors firsthand. As the man and the girl entered the back stairwell, Hendricks shook her head clear and followed Miss Okata through the door at the other end of the room.

"You were right to be suspicious," the woman was saying, when Hendricks snapped out of her daydream about Banke.

"Was I?"

"Oh yes, that will be included in my report to the Misters Grafton. Not that they need outside corroboration on your value. You are, after all, Vice

47

President of Human Resources."

"Director," Hendricks corrected her. "Not Vice President."

"Well, good day to you," said the odd woman. "You have my card if you need anything."

Eleanor Hendricks watched her as she left.

\*\*\*

Ten minutes later, after a quick trip to the bathroom, Abby Adams stood on the balcony that ringed the entire lobby of The Rookery Building. The historic building was magnificent, the Frank Lloyd Wright-designed lobby was a marvel of marble and glass. Abby leaned against a pillar and studied the ceiling as she waited. The blonde wig was gone, her regular black hair was carefully combed. She wore glasses with red plastic rims and a white windbreaker that had been balled up in her large handbag. It showed hardly a wrinkle. Amazing fabrics these days. Her mind wandered to her childhood in Indiana, the sturdy cotton clothes and the heavy farm boots that seemed designed to hold her to the ground. That first feeling of flight, her first gymnastics class, a bright red leotard the most colorful thing her parents had ever bought.

The sound of heavy clomping heels brought her back to herself. She lowered her gaze to find Lionel Banke's illegitimate daughter descending the marvelous curved staircase and then walking toward her, all long legs and big boots, shoulders slumped and casual in a way that only the young can be.

Abby turned and fell into step beside her as they began a circuit of the balcony. It was near the end of the afternoon, on a Friday, and the crowd in the lobby was light. Just enough to make the two of them unremarkable, despite their unusual looks and the odd pairing. It was Chicago, after all. If it wasn't your business, you didn't pay too much attention.

Walking next to her, Abby could feel that the young woman was not as relaxed as she appeared. Subtle waves of tension rolled off her.

"How did it go?" Abby asked.

"Why are you here?" She kept her eyes forward, talking as if to no one.

"I wanted to see how it went."

"I didn't even tell you when I was coming here. How did you know?

Abby shrugged. "This is what I do."

"I saw you in there. Talking to the receptionist. You could have blown the whole thing before it started."

Abby just laughed. The young woman turned and gave her a fierce look. "Never make mistakes, do you? Is that it?"

"How did it go?" Abby asked again, keeping her voice level.

"You're the expert. You tell me."

"Not well."

"That's an understatement." The young woman touched Abby's elbow and steered her to the grand marble staircase that led from the balcony to the lobby. Abby followed her lead as they descended the stairs and crossed the airy lobby. Rather than exit the building, they entered one of the many retail stores on the ground level. They moved through displays and racks of clothes until they stopped in a quiet corner.

"He absolutely refuses to publicly acknowledge me," she blurted, louder than she'd intended, but the store was mostly deserted.

"But privately? He agrees that he's your father?"

She sighed. "He never used those words. Maybe he

thinks I'm trying to secretly record him, but he made it clear that he remembered my mother. I asked him for the money. He refused. I threatened to go public. He laughed and said no one would believe me." Her eyes began to well up with tears. Abby pulled a tissue from one of the outside pockets of her handbag and handed it to the girl.

"He has a wife and three kids," Abby said flatly as she watched the girl smear mascara across her face.

"So?"

"So he's not going to admit it. He's not going to pay you off, either, because you have no power."

"He laughed...I just couldn't believe..." she sobbed again.

"You need to level the playing field."

She pulled the tissue away from her face and looked intently down at Abby. "And you can do that?"

"It's what we do."

"Three million dollars?"

"With five-hundred thousand going to me."

"You can really do it?"

"Did you get what I asked for?"

The young woman reached into her bag and pulled out a Chicago Bears coffee mug. Abby pulled out another tissue, wrapped it around the mug, and then placed it into her own handbag.

"I can do it. Do we have a deal?"

The young woman straightened her shoulders so that she stood at her full five feet, eleven inches. She shoved the tissue in her pocket and held her other hand out to Abby.

"It's a deal," she said.

Abby took her hand.

"Done."

# 6

John Adams leaned back against the waist-high metal fence that surrounded the garden. His legs were crossed at the ankle, his folded arms rested on his chest. His habitual black suit coat was unbuttoned, the pale-yellow dress shirt underneath open at the collar. His eyes were closed. He took a deep breath and held it, elongating his spine and picturing the top of his head rising toward the sky. He continued to hold the breath in. Longer. He listened to the steady sound of a tennis match somewhere nearby. Longer. Then he released it, feeling the tension flow out of his body.

"What the hell?"

Adams opened his eyes at the voice. To his right stood Kirk, the setting sun reflecting off his shaved head. When Kirk saw Adams's eyes were open he gestured toward the towering statue.

"I mean, seriously, what the hell?"

"What do you mean? It's the Scarecrow."

"Yes, I see that." He walked slowly around the base of the twelve-foot statue. "You don't think it's odd?"

Adams uncrossed his legs and stepped forward, his arms still crossed as he walked leisurely over to Kirk.

"Well, no. It's Oz Park. Makes sense to me."

"Yeah, I saw the sign when I came in. I just don't get it. Why bother?"

Adams took another deep, relaxing breath. The fall air was crisp. He looked at the lush plantings all around.

"I could tell you the history of it, but do you really care?"

Kirk laughed.

"Not particularly. You want to meet here, that's fine with me. Chicago I grew up in was a lot rougher than this, is all. Part of Budapest my parents came from, worse. I just don't always feel comfortable in fancy places."

Adams put his hand on the base of the statue, looked around again.

"This part of Chicago used to be pretty blighted. Before my time, nineteen sixties."

"Fucking gentrification."

"I thought you wanted to move into more upscale jobs."

"Sure, stealing from the rich sounds great. I just don't want to socialize with them."

Adams laughed.

"Let's get to business, then." He gestured toward the path and they began walking. "I know you are looking to move out of the rougher trades and into some more rarified jobs."

"I'm thirty-six, man. The violence is getting less attractive every day."

"And it used to be attractive?"

Kirk looked up at the tops of the trees as they walked slowly, then let his head drop.

"Well, yeah, in a way. It sounds crass now I guess, but when I was young, beating someone up—especially someone bigger than me—made me feel good. Strong."

"I can understand that. Not so different than stealing a rich person's car."

"Or ripping off a gambler who cheats."

"Exactly."

"Or robbing a rich person's bank."

"Now you're moving toward the target."

"You need people. I've got skills."

"I understand. But my crew is very small. Family—"

"Mob?"

"No, actual family. Wife, teenage daughter."

"Seriously?"

"My wife's smarter, stronger, and meaner than I am, so don't you worry about that."

"Teenage daughter? That's weird, man."

"It's complicated. She was already an accomplished con artist when we took her in. We're more like guardians than parents. She's closer to a ward, though nobody uses that term anymore except—"

"Batman and Robin."

"Exactly. But she's family, and I trust her completely. Anyway, she does her own thing these days, which means it's just my wife and me. We occasionally hire assistants we trust, but I've been looking for something a little more permanent. I know you don't want to be muscle anymore, but muscle is sometimes necessary, as much as I try to avoid it."

"Like last month with Brock?"

"Yes," Adams grimaced, "that did not go as planned."

"You're a hell of a gambler, though, I'll give you that."

Adams stopped short. Kirk was three steps ahead before he realized it. He turned and looked back to find a strange expression on Adams face.

"I hate gambling." Adams was stern, a dark shadow on his face.

"What?"

"What we do is not gambling. It's the exact opposite of gambling."

He began walking again, faster, and Kirk sped up to keep pace.

"My job," Adams continued, "is to think of every possible action and outcome in a situation and have a plan, and a backup plan, to address it. It's not blackjack, it's chess."

"Okay, but you still bet on the outcome of the chess game, right?"

Adams laughed, a short chuckle, his even white teeth glinting in the sunset. They were approaching the statue of the Tin Man, gleaming gloriously. "True. You're right, and I'm too serious about it. But if it is a bet, I try to make sure the odds are in my favor, and most importantly..."

"Yeah?"

"I make sure that bet is placed with other people's money."

Kirk's laugh was cut short by a man stepping out from behind the statue. He was tall, with distinguished grey temples highlighting his wavy dark hair. He wore an expensive-looking leather jacket, black-framed glasses, and his right hand held a gun.

Kirk took an aggressive step forward, but the man swung the barrel directly at his chest.

"Stop."

Kirk stopped. The man kept the gun on Kirk but looked at Adams.

"Mr. Adams. How ironic to find you talking about other people's money."

"Mr. Allen," Adams said smoothly, his voice level and calm. "I don't think a gun is necessary. Not in a public park. Someone could get hurt."

"Yes, that's the general idea," said Allen. "Park's quiet this time of day, apart from the tennis and the baseball. All the little munchkins are home having their supper."

"Look, Mr. Allen—"

"I want my diamonds!" His voice was a hiss, but his gun hand stayed steady. He seemed to have decided that Kirk was the greater physical threat, and kept the gun pointed at his chest. Kirk, who also thought himself the greatest threat, stood tense, ready to make a move if the opportunity presented itself. It was not the first time, by a long shot, he'd had a gun pointed at him.

"Yes, about that," said Adams.

"I paid you four-hundred thousand dollars to get those diamonds."

"Well, actually, it was only a hundred thousand."

"That's because the rest was due on delivery of the diamonds. Which you did not deliver."

"Yes, of course," Adams continued conversationally. "I can see why that would upset you. I have a friend in the business of buying and selling all manner of things, including diamonds. I took them to him, to make sure we had the real diamonds, and not fakes." Adams shook his head and gave a self-deprecating smile. Kirk noticed that his accent had become a bit more pronounced.

"Of course, they aren't fakes."

"Indeed. My friend offered me three million dollars for them on the spot. It was an offer that was hard to refuse."

Allen was starting to lose his composure. His face had darkened, and Kirk noticed a slight twitch in one eyelid. Kirk shifted his weight slightly forward, to the balls of his feet, ready to spring the instant the gun wavered.

"What did you do with the money, my money!"

Adams spread his hands wide and gave a small shrug. "I gave it to charity. A very worthy cause that helps immigrants."

"That's bullshit."

"Es verdad," said Adams. "It seemed to me that they needed it more than you or Mr. Ackerly or Mrs. Ackerly's pretty neck."

Allen turned the gun from Kirk to Adams.

"I'm going to kill you."

"Come on, Ethan. Little immigrant children. Don't you have a heart?"

"No."

"Maybe you should ask the Wizard for one."

He didn't mean to do it, but Allen couldn't help glance beside him at the tall statue of the Tin Man. That was all Kirk needed to make his move.

He launched himself at the man in one mighty jump, both arms outstretched, his eyes on the gun hand. Allen swung the gun around, but not in time. Kirk's hands grasped Allen's wrist, turning outward, and the rest of his body barreled shoulder-first into Allen's torso.

Kirk was surprised, however, as Allen shifted his weight and twisted his body, redirecting Kirk's momentum past him and head-first into the stone pedestal of the Tin Man statue. Kirk's brain flooded with light before the pain, which followed close behind, screamed through his head. He fell to the ground. Somewhere in the part of his consciousness that was still functioning, he heard a gunshot, grunting, a shout of pain, another gunshot, then silence.

With great effort, Kirk pushed himself up onto his hands and knees, opened his eyes enough to see blood streaming down from his forehead onto the mulch in front of him. Before he could think of his next move, his body took over and he threw up, an unpleasant and clearly recognizable regurgitation of the short rib goulash he'd had earlier at The Little Bucharest. He put his left hand up to his wet forehead, pressed hard, and then sat slowly back on his heels, head tilted toward the sky. He took his time; if he was going to be shot it would have happened already.

"Here." Adams stepped into his view, holding a white handkerchief out to him.

"Who the fuck carries a handkerchief?" moaned Kirk, grabbing it and pressing it on his forehead.

Adams laughed. "Are you okay?"

Kirk turned his body toward him, lost his balance and fell backward on his ass. Adams had his suit coat off, and it was tied around his left forearm in an untidy bundle. In his right hand he held Allen's pistol down against his thigh.

"Can you get up?"

"What the hell happened?"

"Later. There'll be cops any minute. Can you get up?" Adams looked around quickly, then tucked the gun in his waistband at the small of his back. He reached out his free hand and grabbed Kirk's, helping to pull him to his feet.

"Where'd he go?" Asked Kirk, looking at the bloodstained walkway and then turning a full circle to scan the park.

"He's gone," Adams assured him.

"But you've got his gun."

"I do."

"Like magic."

"Just lucky."

"Like the fucking Wizard of Oz."

# 7

Abby heard an unfamiliar voice when she and Suki entered the apartment. She gave her a quick look and held a finger to her lips, moved her quickly out of sight into the hallway and then into the second bedroom.

"I'll come get you in a minute," she whispered. The young woman nodded and sat on the bed.

Back in the hallway, Abby moved as close as she could while remaining out of sight.

"Right, but where'd the knife come from?"

"I don't know," said Adams. "After you distracted him, I kicked the gun out of his hand. It went off when it hit the ground. I looked up, there was a knife in his hand. Amazingly fast, the guy's what, fifty?"

"Younger than fifty, but yeah."

"He comes at me, and I just get my forearm up in time. Hurts like a bastard and I fall down. Come up with the gun off the pavement but he's already over the fence and into the trees. I shot at him once but I'm not a great shot, and there were a lot of trees."

"Jesus, man."

"I didn't want to shoot anymore, better to get out of there quick. I know how to find him."

"Make him pay."

"*Si.*"

"Well, count me in," said the voice.

Abby rounded the corner to find Adams and the other man seated at the long table. The card castle had collapsed, leaving playing cards scattered everywhere. The guy was white, in his mid-thirties, with a shaved head and a trim beard. One big, muscled arm was raised, and his hand held an ice pack to his forehead. A snake tattoo slithered up the side of his neck. Her husband sat next to him, trying to tape a big gauze bandage to his own forearm using only one hand.

"What have you done now?!" she asked as she crossed into the room, her voice loud.

The other man jumped, but Adams put his hand on his shoulder, dropping the roll of gauze in the process.

"It's all right. This is my wife, Abby."

Blood was dripping on the floor, and Abby changed direction toward the open kitchen, grabbing a dish towel and soaking it in the sink.

"Abby, this is Mr. Kirk," said Adams as if everything was perfectly normal.

"Call me Jacob, please."

Abby crossed to stand in from of them, dropped the towel on the floor and used her booted foot to move it across the blood. At the same time, she reached forward and pulled the ice pack away from Kirk's forehead.

"Ouch, that had to hurt. What hit you?"

"He had a fight with a statue," said Adams, and gave an uncharacteristic giggle. Kirk started laughing as well.

"Jesus, are you drunk?"

"No, actually," said John, "but it's not a bad idea. What have we got?"

"Nothing. It's six o'clock, we're supposed to be having a logistics meeting."

He sighed.

"It's Friday, love, let's give it a rest."

She pulled the gauze away from his forearm, without gentleness, making him wince as the tape pulled the hair on his skin. "Oh hush, this is nothing."

"It's not nothing. It was a knife."

"It's just a scratch. Let me guess, was it Allen?"

Adams looked to the side at the scattered playing cards, stayed silent.

"I knew it!" She leaned down and picked up the wet towel, threw it across the room, over the dividing counter, and into one of the two kitchen sinks where it hit with a splat. "Jesus, John. I knew we should have played that one straight. He wasn't just any sucker."

John looked back at her. "It's not a big deal."

"It is. And I expect that you will fix it."

"Don't be so bossy—"

"Why not?" she said over him. "I'm the boss."

"Are you?" asked Kirk, who'd been watching the exchange carefully.

"What?" It seemed like she had forgotten he was even there.

"Are you the boss," he repeated, standing, "because I'm interested in a job."

She faced him squarely, then purposely looked him up and down where he stood, head to toe and back again. She took a deep breath and turned back to John.

"This is the guy you were talking about?"

"Yes. I had a meeting arranged with him this afternoon."

"You brought him here?"

"It wasn't my intention, but we needed to get off the street quickly, and get first aid."

"You've pretty much given him the job, now that he knows where we are. Either that or we kill him."

Kirk raised his eyebrows and took a step back.

"She's kidding," said John, who stood and began gathering the playing cards, thinking they would need the table for the meeting.

Kirk looked back at Abby, unconvinced.

She sighed and slumped her shoulders. She ran a hand through her short black hair. It had just a touch of

60

premature gray running through it.

"I'm kidding. Go get another ice pack, there are more in the freezer."

***

Ten minutes later they were seated at the long table, John at one end and Abby and Kirk on either side. They had seltzer water and pretzels. John was starting to build a new card house as Abby talked. Kirk wished they were serving something a bit stronger to drink.

"John is obsessed with upping the game," continued Abby. "Each job has to be bigger than the last or he gets bored."

"It's not boredom," said John, without looking up. "I don't know what it is." He finished placing one card and picked up another, turning to Kirk. "It's like a countdown clock. I want to have an impact on the world, do something that makes a difference, and I feel like time is running out."

"You're not old," said Abby. Her voice was the warmest Kirk had heard it yet.

"Not me," John said. "It's the world that's running out of time. Everyone's just going on as usual as if we weren't about to drive the planet off the edge of a cliff."

Kirk swallowed his pretzel before speaking, trying to make sure his manners were up to snuff. "And you save the world by stealing stuff?"

"You'd be surprised," said Abby.

"We've used shell corporations to give more than thirty-five million dollars to anti-poverty and pro-environment groups over the last ten years."

Kirk's jaw dropped. Literally, like a cartoon, his mouth fell open. If he hadn't swallowed his pretzel it would have fallen out onto the table.

61

"You stole thirty-five..."

"Million," confirmed John. "No, that's just what we donated, but it's not enough. This country operates on billions of dollars a day. What we do is a drop in the bucket."

"And you..."

"Gave it away, yes, that's what I said."

"Well, not all of it," Abby interrupted, waving her arm at the luxurious apartment. "But most."

Kirk's mind was reeling. He thought first of his mother, who had come from Budapest to escape an abusive husband, who had worked in some of the worst, most grueling laundries in Chicago to put food on the table. His own hard-fought childhood, brawling on the street corner over lunch money. He wasn't a big kid, so he worked out in their cramped apartment, using old gallon milk jugs filled with water as barbells, nailing a broken broom handle to the door frame as a pull-up bar. He had risen to the top of his neighborhood gang to better his life, and still he only made four or five grand a month. In June they had pulled a bank robbery that netted fifty for each of them, a hundred grand for Kirk as the mastermind and leader. It was that success that had given him thoughts of bigger scores, led him to asking questions in dubious places, until he came across O'Brian, who had mentioned his friend Adams who pulled big-time con jobs, had pretended to only half listen as O'Brian told him about Adams at Wrigley field, about Adams liking to play cards at a certain place...

"I'm in," he blurted, while the man, improbably named John Adams, was still speaking. Now that he thought of it, that was almost certainly not his real name.

"Excuse me?"

"I said I'm in, I want to help. With the charities."

"Right," said Abby. Her heavily made up face showed

62

skepticism. "The charities."

Now that Kirk was thinking about her face, he felt self-conscious staring, but had trouble looking away. She was good looking, about his age, obviously smart. Why all the makeup? Stop staring, he thought. Snap out of it.

"Well, of course I like the idea of being rich," he said earnestly. "You'd know I was lying if I said I didn't. But I can see where you're coming from. Totally. My childhood wasn't that great. You'd think, since then, there'd have been some progress on making Chicago a better place for poor families, but really, it's just as bad as ever. I could think of plenty of good uses for rich people's money. Besides," he smiled, "you do keep some of it, right?"

"Usually about ten percent," she said.

Kirk did the math in his head and liked the sum.

"But," John broke in, "what we really need is muscle, and you said you wanted to get out of that."

"Depends," said Kirk, still doing arithmetic.

"We'd need someone who can hire and manage muscle, we've never really worked as more than a duo or trio."

"I know guys. I can find guys. But they don't have special skills. Well, one guy, Alexander, is really good with locks. You'd never know he'd been there. But, mostly, just some tough guys. Is that the kind of guy you're going to need?"

"It is," Abby assured him. "We've been looking at hitting the financial district. Electronically."

"We're not hackers ourselves," said John, starting on the fifth story of his card tower. "Too old to learn new tricks, but we've got contacts." He released the card and it stayed in place. "It's not about what you can break in and carry out anymore—"

"Though that's still my favorite kind of job," Abby interrupted.

"It's about what you can siphon off when no one is looking," Adams finished. He picked up another deck of cards and started to shuffle them languidly.

"If it's all cyber, what do you need the muscle for?"

"Well," said John. He leaned forward and flipped the top four cards of the deck over and laid them in front of Kirk. They were all aces. "Sometimes you need help getting in..." He dealt the next four cards face up as well; they were all jacks. "And sometimes the way to make sure they aren't looking at you is to give them something else to look at."

He dealt another card, but so hard that it slid and spun down the length of the table. Kirk watched it go, and when he turned back to John the four aces and four jacks that had been on the table in front of him were gone. Disappeared.

He smiled and looked at John, then at Abby.

"Fuck, yeah," he said. Which meant he was all in.

# 8

"So, what's the job?"

"We haven't decided yet," said Adams.

"Actually..."

A knowing look passed between them.

"She signed on?"

Abby nodded.

"Excellent." He turned toward Kirk. "We are definitely going to need you for this one, if you're up for it."

"How much are we talking about?" said Kirk, trying not to appear too eager. He had worked a long time for something like this.

"I told her three million," said Abby.

"Thirty million," said John.

"Wow, that's..." began Kirk.

"Not what we talked about, John. She said three million, we keep five hundred thousand."

"I know what the proposal was," Adams replied, taking a sip of his water, "and we will honor that. We'll steal the three million from her father, and then another twenty-seven from the rest of Grafton Corp."

"Grafton Corp?" exclaimed Kirk, nearly choking on his drink. "Even I've heard of Grafton Corp, and I know shit-all about the financial sector. Hard to miss all the commercials, how I should invest all my extra cash with them. Which supposes I have cash to begin with."

"I don't think it's a good idea—" Abby started to say.

"Exactly why they're the perfect target," John said, waving his hand with enthusiasm and ignoring Abby's interjection. "They are making money for people who have lots of money. That's their only reason to be. More money for people with money. Might as well be their slogan." He turned to look at his wife. "Abby, love, this is what I've been working toward, all this time. This is the real thing."

She sat quietly for a moment, playing idly with the napkin in front of her.

"If we do this," she began, looking at them each in turn, "she can't know."

"Of course not."

"Seriously, as far as she's concerned, it's her daddy's three million and that's it."

"Of course," John said again.

"That means the tech has to be perfect. No one can know about it until we are long out of there and gone. All settled up, with her on her way to whatever country she's planning to go to when it's over."

"Got it."

"Can you do that?" asked Kirk. "I mean, I'm not doubting you or anything, I just want to know what I'm getting into."

"No, that's fine," John reassured him. "I have to talk to my connection, but I'm sure it's going to work. He has a new guy who's just doing amazing things. Are you sure you want in?"

"What would my cut be?"

"One third of ten percent," said Abby, who was clearly the business mind of the pair. "After expenses, which includes a hundred thousand for each of your men that we can depend on, and whatever Don charges us for the tech."

That seemed to Kirk like it would still be at least a million dollars for him, all said and done. And that was at the very least. He had a few ideas about where this would go and what it might lead to. All the possibilities looked a hell of a lot better than robbing Osco drug stores.

"I'm definitely in."

"Excellent," said John. He gave them both a warm, confident smile. "When do we meet her?" he asked Abby.

"Now," said Abby. "She's waiting in the other room."

\*\*\*

Abby opened the door to the bedroom. "You ready?"

The young woman put down the copy of *Blanche on the Lam* she was reading and jumped off the bed. "Yeah."

"Sure you're all set?"

"Absolutely."

"Anything you want to go over?"

Suki bristled and pushed past Abby. "I'm ready."

"Okay, okay."

They rounded the corner into the living area and both Adams and Kirk rose to their feet.

"Hi," she said, "I'm Suki." She extended her hand toward Kirk. "You must be Mr. Adams."

"Actually, I'm Mr. Kirk, but you can call me Jacob."

Adams stepped forward. "I'm John, pleased to meet you." He motioned toward a chair. "Can I get you anything?"

"Whatever you're having is fine," she said, sitting at the table. Kirk retook his seat and Abby pulled out a chair and sat next to Suki, who was looking at the five-story house of cards at the end of the table.

Kirk took the opportunity to give her the once-over while she wasn't paying attention. She was African American, with dark skin and long hair in tight braids. She was wearing a sweatshirt with rhinestones across the collarbone and when she first entered the room, he had noticed her artfully torn jeans and expensive boots. She caught him looking and smiled. Her teeth were bright and perfectly even, and she had a little jewel stud in her nose. He guessed that she was maybe seventeen or eighteen, but it was hard to say.

She held his gaze until he looked away, reaching for his drink but hitting the card tower with the back of his hand, causing it to collapse.

"Shit, sorry John."

Adams returned to the table and set a coaster in front of Suki, placing a glass on it.

"Don't worry about it; they aren't supposed to be permanent." He sat at the head of the table and picked up one of the decks that was lined up on the table, a blue and white diamond pattern on the back, shuffled it a few times, and then fanned it out in front of Suki. "Pick a card."

She did and showed it to Abby. It was the queen of spades.

"Show Jacob as well," Adams told her. She did. He held out the deck again and she put the card back in. He shuffled the deck several times then set it down on the corner of the table.

Suki took a drink and grimaced. "This is club soda."

"What did you think it was?" asked Abby.

"I don't know, gin and tonic?"

"How old are you?" asked Kirk.

"Old enough, pal."

"Relax," said Adams, making a calming motion with his hand. "Let's move on to business."

Suki raised her eyebrows. "What about the trick?"

"Later. Right now, I want to get us on topic. As this is Jacob's first meeting, we'll fill him in a bit on what you've asked us to do, and then let you know what we have planned." He nodded at Abby.

"Suki's father is Lionel Banke," Abby began. "Do you know who that is?"

68

"Yeah," Kirk nodded. "TV commercials for investments. I'm not a huge football fan myself, but I remember him, and Refrigerator Perry, and Harbaugh. I was about eight years old."

"Banke's wife is not Suki's mother. In fact, Banke will not admit in public that Suki is any relation at all."

"But in private?"

"Yeah." Suki looked solemn. "I managed to confront him this spring. I had sent him letters, phone calls. Nothing. Finally, I cornered him on the street when he was leaving work one day."

"And he admitted it?" It was nothing that Kirk would have done, that's for sure. For some reason, in her company, that knowledge made him embarrassed. He looked away, touched the bandage on his forehead, studied the windows.

"When I said her name, you could see it on his face. He said she was nobody, nothing to him, and he wasn't my father. Said I was just gold digging."

"Who is your mother?" Kirk asked.

"Nobody. She nothin'."

"I'm sure that's not true," Adams said gently.

"It is!" She looked up with wide, flaming eyes. "And it's his fault. Havin' me ruined her. I almost killed her, she needed time off, lost her job, started using." Her eyes began to fill, and Adams took a clean white handkerchief from his pocket and handed it to her.

Jesus, thought Kirk, how many of those things does he carry?

"Let's talk about what we can do for you," Abby said brightly. "I think that's much more fun to focus on."

"Right," Suki said, wiping her eyes. "Fun. Three million dollars buys a lot of fun."

"Hell yeah," Kirk agreed.

"The funny thing is," Suki went on, passing the

handkerchief back to Adams, "I didn't want any money from him, not until he rejected me. Then I sent him a letter asking for two hundred thousand dollars to pay for college. I never heard back. After that I met a woman who gave me your card. I was doing her nails, I have a part-time job doin' that, and we got to talking. Somehow it all came out, and she said you'd helped her out with her husband."

"And we're going to help you too, dear," said Abby,

"How are you so sure? Just the three of you?"

"We have some friends, if we need them," John assured her. "But we usually don't. We'll have a better idea after we review the surveillance."

"Surveillance?" asked Kirk.

"Yes," said Abby. "I planted a bug on the Grafton mainframe when I was there today. Not only will it gather information, but it will test to see how good their cyber security is. If they don't notice it by go time next week, we'll know our plan will work."

"Wait a minute." Suki had a confused look on her face. "You did that today? You didn't even know if I was going to hire you or not."

"We knew," said John. "That's why we're good at what we do." He took the top card off the deck in front of him and laid it face down in front of Suki. She looked down to see the queen of spades staring back up at her.

Kirk's eyes widened, but Suki seemed unimpressed.

"Is that how you think you're going to take down Lionel Banke? Tricks?"

John Adams kept his voice soft and even.

"Do you know the best way to level the playing field, Suki? Most people, in the middle of a high-stakes game, will use every trick they can think of to give themselves an edge." He picked up the deck of cards again and shuffled it, set it down and fanned it out into one long, perfectly spaced arc. "But they get it wrong. The best way to level the playing field is to play your tricks before the game even begins." He flicked his hand and the deck flipped from face down to face up. Every single card was the queen of spades.

# 9

Mid-day on Tuesday, Jacob Kirk found himself strolling through the Shedd Aquarium, a place he hadn't been since he visited on a grade-school field trip more than twenty years earlier. As if on cue, a gaggle of ten-year-olds raced past, followed by a haggard-looking teacher who made feeble attempts to quiet and slow them. He watched them go by.

Kirk was there with John and Abby to meet Danny O'Brian and get the piece of computer trickery they would need for the Grafton heist.

When he looked back, Abby was holding an envelope out to him.

"What's this?"

"Little present," she said, and gave him a smile. John walked along beside her, his attention absorbed by the two manta rays gliding by in the tank next to them.

Kirk opened the envelope and unfolded the enclosed sheet of paper. It took him a minute to realize what he was looking at, and when it finally made sense, he stopped short.

"I don't understand..."

"We had to look into your background, Jacob, if we're going to be partners. I hope you don't mind."

Kirk's eyes were still riveted to the bottom of the page, and the signature there: Jimmy Colatano. He couldn't believe it.

"You got me off the hook with Jimmy C.?" He looked up at them. Who the hell were these people? "You two are connected?"

"No," said Abby, putting her hand on his forearm. "Of course not. Not to the Colatanos anyway. We've got a close friend who's related to someone with a good deal of pull with that family. Owed us a favor."

Kirk folded the paper and put it back in the envelope.

"You gotta understand," he said, drawing close and talking low, "I tried to pay this off, in cash. It's only ten grand, but Jimmy wouldn't take it. Wanted it paid in trade. Stuff I didn't want to do. He's been holding it over me for years."

"Well, now he won't be," said John with a smile.

Kirk folded the envelope and put it in the back pocket of his jeans. He looked at them both and smiled. "Thank you."

"*De nada*," said John, but a moment later the smile fell from his face as something behind Kirk caught his eye.

Kirk turned around and looked down the long glass tunnel that ran through the enormous tank. At the other end a man was striding their way. He was tall with wavy black hair and black-framed glasses, and he was flanked on either side by a muscular man, neither of whom seemed particularly interested in the fish.

"Shit," whispered Kirk. "Is that Allen?"

"It's not Steve Zissou," said Abby wryly. "Let's get out of here."

They turned as one and headed in the opposite direction, taking the first available turn.

"Excuse me, sir?"

John and Jacob both turned to look at the woman who had called to them from across the open room. She wore a grey pantsuit and had brown hair streaked with blonde. She was walking aggressively toward them in a manner that screamed one word to Kirk: cop.

John grabbed Kirk by the elbow and swung him away

from the woman and toward a service door on the other side of the room.

"Didn't expect to see her here," he said as he pushed Kirk toward the door.

"Sir," the woman said more loudly. "Ma'am. I'd like to talk to you for a minute if I could."

"Adams!" Allen had exited the tunnel and was now walking swiftly into the room, nearly colliding with Levesque, who turned indignantly to see who was getting in her way.

Jacob didn't see what happened after that because Abby closed the door hard behind them and threw the deadbolt on it. John had already broken into a trot in front of him.

"What now?" asked Jacob as Abby brushed past him and broke into a jog.

"Run," she called back over her shoulder.

***

Suki sat in the old Lincoln, drumming her fingers on the steering wheel. It seemed like all they ever did was ask her to wait around. No mistake, they'd been really good to her, but when this was over, she'd be glad to be on her own again, doing her own thing. They were so...married. Kirk was interesting, though. But old. Like thirty-something.

She looked across again at the weird statue of the man and the fish. Drummed her fingers again, looked expectantly at the side entrance. Nothing. Someone would ask her to move along soon, to clear the zone designated as "Passenger Loading Only." She peered through the trees, knowing there was a hotdog cart just over there somewhere. A quick check of her jeans pocket yielded a ten-dollar bill. Fate.

She hopped out of the car and started up the walk alongside the Shedd Aquarium, turned left and there it was: Kim and Carlo's Hotdog Cart. It seemed to be calling her name. No, wait, that was someone actually calling her name. She turned to see Abby, John, and Jacob racing down the front steps toward her, shouting. John was gesturing wildly toward the car, an angry look on his face. Angry at her.

She raced back, meeting them halfway to the car, turning to run with them.

"Why are we running?" she yelled.

"Just run!" Abby shouted.

So she ran, until they were about fifty feet from the car, when it suddenly exploded.

\*\*\*

"What the fuck!" shouted Kirk.

Suki had her hands over her ears and was screaming. The old car had lifted completely off the ground and landed upside down, flames were shooting up from it, and black smoke was being whisked away by wind from the lake.

Abby grabbed Suki by the upper arm and hauled her away from the car. John looked back the way they came, but no one was following them.

"Quickly!" he pointed through a few trees to a small parking lot, probably for employees. "We need transport." He grabbed Suki's other arm, but she shrugged them both off, running on her own steam.

The four of them crossed the street and entered the parking lot.

"That one!" shouted John, pointing at a big black SUV a few rows over.

"You think it's going to have keys in it?" Jacob asked,

incredulous, but John was already pulling a small leather case from his inside pocket.

"Don't need keys," he said, but was interrupted by the wail of a police siren.

"No time!" shouted Abby, then pointed. "There!"

Idling at the curb on the edge of the lot was a school bus, exhaust pumping from its tailpipe. The kids were all in the aquarium and the bus driver was sitting on the curb smoking a cigarette, looking at his phone.

"That's a terrible idea," said John, mostly to himself because the others had already turned and begun sprinting for the bus.

Suki, who had been closest, rushed past the driver and leaped up the stairs and into the bus.

"Hey!" the driver shouted. He began to rise but Kirk gave him a stiff arm as he and Abby ran by, sending the poor man sprawling on the pavement, his phone smashing and skittering away. The bus started to pull away just as they climbed onto it, first Abby, then Kirk. Hanging on to the handrail, he leaned out and looked back to see John about thirty feet behind, and about a hundred yards behind him a police car coming around the corner of the Field Museum, lights flashing and siren screaming.

"Go!" John was shouting, waving them forward as he drew level with the doorway, racing to keep up with the accelerating school bus. Kirk reached out his left hand, still holding the handrail with his right, and leaned out until he could grasp John by the wrist, hauling him up onto the bus.

They rushed up the three steps to the main aisle, which is when John first realized Suki was driving the bus.

"Oh no, no no no," he said, shaking his head, "definitely not—" but he was cut off when the front of the bus hit the curb and launched onto the sidewalk in front of the aquarium. He and Kirk went sprawling backward, scrabbling at the seat backs to stay upright.

"I see another one!" shouted Abby, who had run to the back of the bus and was looking out the rear emergency door.

"Suki," gasped John, pulling himself upright. "Let me drive!"

"No time," she shouted, and hung a hard left onto a pedestrian pathway that led between the aquarium and the lake. People enjoying the early afternoon sun scattered in all directions.

"They're following us!" shouted Abby.

Kirk, meanwhile, had pulled a pistol out of the back of his jeans.

"What the hell are you going to do with that?" asked Adams over the noise of the horn that Suki was pushing relentlessly.

"Slow 'em down a bit," he said and stepped onto one of the seats halfway down the bus so that he could get at the window.

John turned back to the front window. He saw only the blue water of the lake.

"This doesn't go anywhere!"

"I see that now," Suki responded without looking back. She was having a hard time avoiding the pedestrians and the random trash cans and park benches.

In fact, the path did go somewhere. It hugged the rounded edge of the aquarium until it came out the other side into a green space at the back of the Field Museum. Kirk was afraid there would be a police car waiting for them at the far end, but there was only the one pursuing them.

"I thought you were going to slow them down," John shouted.

"I'm trying. I can't open this fucking window."

"You need to pull the little things."

"What things?"

"There's one on each side, stick your fingers in and slide them."

"You. Have. Got. To. Be. Kidding. Me!" Kirk couldn't do it without putting down his gun, and he didn't want to put down his gun.

Just then the police cruiser found daylight and sped up beside them.

"Hang on!" Suki yelled just as the bus lurched hard to the right, forcing the police car to swerve into a row of bushes.

"Nice one, Suki!" cheered Abby, as she ran back to the front of the bus. "Keep going," she said, pointing ahead to where the path dipped down to go under Lake Shore Drive. "There will be more soon. There's always more."

As they rocketed toward the tunnel, fear rose in Kirk's throat. "Can we fit through that?"

"Only one way to find out!" shouted Suki, actually laughing a second later as they barely fit beneath the overpass.

"Slow down," yelled Abby as they burst from the other side to find the pathway took a near ninety-degree turn to the right.

The bus skidded, Suki wrenching the wheel as hard as she could. Abby grabbed it as well, pulling with all her strength. Kirk and Adams were flung sideways into the seats as the back of the bus fishtailed around, leaving the path momentarily and crashing through some greenery before returning to the pavement.

They regained control of the bus just as they approached a hard turn to the left that led to a long pedestrian bridge crossing the railroad tracks toward Michigan Ave.

"Slower," commanded Abby, and Suki obeyed, bringing them down to ten miles per hour. "Get off," she shouted, and grabbed Suki by the arm. She pushed her down the steps, taking her place behind the wheel. "All of you, off."

John immediately did what she said, and Kirk decided not to argue. The three of them hopped off one after another, landing nimbly on the grass. Kirk looked back at the bus to see Abby also jump off just as the bus entered the causeway. She jogged toward them without looking back at the big yellow vehicle, which was now coasting across the bridge.

"In the trees," she hissed, indicating the greenery off to the side.

They moved quickly through it and out the other side to the sidewalk where cars were parked along Columbus, Suki laughing all the way.

"Stop laughing," whispered John. They could still hear the siren of the cruiser, stuck in the bushes.

"I can't," Suki gasped. "That was fucking awesome."

Kirk started laughing as well and Abby shot him a look as they approached a grey Toyota Corolla. John was already taking his little kit out again.

"What?" Kirk said, trying not to laugh.

"You couldn't even open the goddamn window," she said, the side of her mouth twitching.

"Get in." John had opened the driver's door and pushed the button to unlock the rest.

"It's made for grade-school kids," Abby added, and this time she couldn't hold the laugh in. John hot-wired the engine and started the car as Suki and Kirk were now laughing wildly.

"Put your seatbelts on." He was scowling.

"C'mon John, it's funny."

"I don't find it funny."

He would have peeled out to make his point, but they were trying to avoid attention, so instead he drove quietly off toward the apartment, his hands gripping the wheel tightly.

# 10

Suki flopped down on the sofa and let out an extra giggle. John Adams strode through the space and opened the sliding door to the balcony so hard it nearly shattered. He took a deep breath.

"Please stop laughing. It's not funny."

"Hey," said Kirk, coming to her defense, "it's just nerves."

John rounded on him.

"You think it's funny, too? I didn't see you wearing gloves on that bus."

"What's that supposed to mean?"

"Prints," said Abby, who had gone straight into the open kitchen to get a drink of water. "Do the police have your prints on file?"

"Of course they have his prints, Abby. You don't run a gang in Dunning and not get printed at least once."

Kirk wanted to interject, but he was absolutely correct.

Abby set her glass of water on the divider bar and pulled her phone out of the back pocket of her black pants. "I'll take care of it." She moved off into the bedroom with the phone to her ear.

Kirk watched her go, his stress level beginning to rise now that the adrenaline was wearing off. He spun back to John. "What does that mean?"

"She knows someone who can take care of it."

"Cops?"

"No, not cops, but someone who makes a pretty convincing cop when he wants to. And is good at making things disappear."

"He's going to make a school bus disappear?" asked Suki, still grinning.

"That would be great," said Abby, returning to the room, "but probably just the prints."

John pulled a chair away from the table, set it in front of the sofa, and sat facing Suki. He leaned forward with his elbows on his knees and looked at her intently. Her smile faded at the look on his face.

"You," he said softly, "are not supposed to be part of the job. You hired us to do it for you. You need to stay out of it, for your own safety."

Suki was not going to let that go easily.

"I hired you, so I'm the boss. I'm in charge of the job."

"No," John said, raising his index finger in front of her. "You are in charge of picking the job, I'm in charge of running the job."

"John," said Abby softly.

"Wait. Let me finish." He looked back at Suki. "You have no training in this, you could get yourself killed. Your only job was to wait in the car, and that was only because we had to make a quick stop to pick something up. But sometimes things go wrong. The aquarium was a setup, the person I was expecting to make a deal with was not there. Some very bad people were waiting there for us instead. We come out in a hurry, and where are you? You're going to get a hotdog."

That was enough for Suki. She batted his pedantic wagging finger out of the way and stuck her own pointing finger in his face.

"If I stayed in the car, I'd be fucking blown up now, wouldn't I?"

"That's actually a good point," said Kirk from over by the window.

"I didn't ask you," said John.

"But he's right," said Abby. John stood and faced her

as she came around the end of the bar and crossed the room. "You have to cut her some slack, she was almost killed."

"Sheer luck she's not," added Kirk, who didn't like to be told to shut up.

"I don't want her on the job," John said, ignoring everything else. His voice was low but intent. "She's just a kid."

"I'm not—"

"And we need her to be safe, because we can't do the Grafton heist without her." He turned and looked at Suki. "Or do you want to just give us the print now, so we can do the job without you?"

"What print?" asked Kirk.

Suki was in no way cowed.

"If you do the job without me, how do I know you wouldn't just keep the money for yourself? I don't even know your name. It sure as hell isn't John Adams."

John whirled around on Abby. "You see? She's no fool. We're not a chummy family, and she's not our daughter."

"I never said she was." Abby's voice was rising dangerously.

"You've been acting like it. Hanging out all weekend, shopping together..."

"We were getting things for the job!"

She was toe-to-toe with him now. Suki got up off the couch and moved a few feet back, out of the potential blast area if one of them spontaneously combusted.

"And do you always take the client along when you do that? I'm surprised you haven't asked her to move into the apartment." He was shouting now. "We have a bedroom that's not being used."

"You shut your mouth!" Abby screamed back at him. She turned on her heel and marched to the door, turning back with her hand on the handle. "You never think anything is your fault, John." Her voice was calmer now. Suki looked from one of them to the other, then grabbed her bag and followed Abby out the door, clicking it shut behind her.

There was a pause, and then Kirk clapped his hands together in the awkward silence.

"Soooo, beer?"

John put a wan smile on his face. "I'm sorry, it's just, sometimes...we're just having a few problems."

"Performance issues?"

John furrowed his brow. "What are you talking about, that's none of your business." He sat heavily on the sofa.

Kirk laughed, moving to the kitchen and opening the refrigerator. There was no beer.

"Not sex, man, business." He leaned on the counter and looked across the room at John, who had a defeated set to his shoulders. "Honestly," Kirk continued, "I'm worried, man. I got into this because I heard you two were something special."

Adams straightened up and turned his full attention on Kirk, his face showing surprise at this new edge to Kirk's voice.

"I mean, I've known you a few weeks and so far, you've blown a poker scam, you've been ambushed in a public park, and a simple pickup from a source went so badly that your car was blown up!" He said the last part with emphasis, like twisting a knife.

Adams stood up.

"I have everything under control."

"Do you? Because I could have been in that car when it blew up. The girl and your wife could have been in that car when it blew up."

"We did this job, last month, and the client was unhappy with how it went."

"Right, I met him. And if I remember right, he was

unhappy because you kept all the diamonds you stole for him."

"He was not going to put them to good use."

"Even so—"

"Spare me the lecture. It's nothing we haven't done before, but this man, Allen, he had some deep connections we didn't know about. Organized connections, and he was able to find us that way. But, I have it all taken care of now."

"Right, your friend with the connections. It didn't look like you had it under control at the aquarium. I want to believe you," Kirk added quickly, raising both hands. "But I have to think of the risk."

"About a million dollars, after all is said and done."

"Which doesn't do me any good if I'm dead, or in jail."

Adams moved to the door. "I've got to do some things. You can trust me or not, but I know this plan will work. I can see it laid out from beginning to end. Everything else, just hiccups. Help yourself to some food, whatever. I'll be back later."

Kirk watched him leave, then turned and looked around the large room. Help yourself to whatever, Adams had said. He'd have a good look around. Adams was right, it was a good plan, well thought out. He could even see the beauty of giving most of the money to charity. A good way to stick it to the rich assholes, and hell, a man only needs so much money, right? Right?

# 11

Dajuan Campbell looked up from the motorcycle he was working on to see Suki crossing the floor of the auto body shop. The girl had muscles like you wouldn't believe—martial arts training, he knew. But she was soft in lots of places, too. Lots of really great places. He had met her a few weeks ago, when she came in just like this, looking around.

"You Dajuan?" she had asked him.

"For you I am."

"I'm sorry," the sexy girl had said. She looked about seventeen, with cornrows and clothes that were expensive yet club-ready. "I thought this was a business, not some pickup joint." She turned on the heel of her tall black boots and strode toward the door. She was only five four but to Dajuan she looked like an African goddess.

"It is," he said. He stood hastily and wiped his hands on a rag. "I am. Dajuan. This is my business."

She looked around at the motorcycles and the half-dozen cars in the warehouse space.

"This your only business?"

"What's that mean?"

"I heard from my friend Clarice that you did some other things here. Darker things."

Dajuan's smile never faltered. When he started making real cash, the first thing he did was to get his teeth fixed, finally, and he never missed an opportunity to show them off. They shone like the gold necklaces he wore, three or four on any given day, depending on his mood. The necklaces were short, almost like collars, so that they wouldn't hang into the machinery. He'd seen that happen to a guy once at Oscar's, nearly lost half his face.

"I heard real dark things. Drugs, trafficking," she went on. He didn't react, but his smile disappeared. "I'm not here for none of that; I disapprove. Handsome man like you shouldn't be subjugating women; makes you ugly."

"Well, I can assure you I have no business concerns like the ones you describe. I'm an honorable mechanic." He looked around to be sure all the others were in the back. It was just the two of them. He moved away from the motorcycle and over to the tool rack, opened a drawer and removed something that looked like a long black paddle. "I am, however, going to have to ask you to take off your jacket."

Suki stared back at him.

"If you know Clarice," he shrugged, "I'm sure she told you I like to be careful."

She dropped her handbag off her shoulder and onto the concrete floor and unzipped her jacket, which was black leather with gold studs worked all over it in a swirling pattern. It had black fringe coming off the cuffs. She opened it slowly to reveal a simple white T-shirt with no bra underneath, slid the jacket down her shoulders and handed it to him.

Without a word, he pushed a button on the paddle and ran it up and down her coat. Then, still holding the coat by the collar, he ran the paddle up and down in front of her body, then bent to run it around the outside of her bag. Straightening up, he made a twirling motion with the paddle and she turned slowly until she was facing away from him, looking out the open garage door at the far end of the space, where the sun was setting over a 7-Eleven.

Dajuan studied her from behind. Her ass and thighs were muscular and stuffed tightly into a pair of old jeans. Her black leather boots had almost no heels. She was a woman who wanted to be able to move when she wanted to move. A hooker would have had two or three inches of heel, at least. She was maybe some other kind of hustler, though. He wasn't so stupid as to disregard his usual precautions. He and Clarice weren't on speaking terms, not for a while, so he couldn't really verify that angle. Best to just take it slow, see what developed.

"Good?" she asked, turning back around as he set the paddle on the workbench.

"Gotta be careful," he said, handing her back the leather jacket. She put it on again, zipping it enough to cover her chest.

"Guess so."

"So. You don't like me but you're here. What is it you want..."

"Suki," she said. "You can call me Suki."

"Pretty. Why are you here, Suki? Not that I don't love having you. I just got things that need doing."

She picked up her bag and unzipped it, fished with her right hand and brought out two brick sized objects, setting them on the workbench. They were credit cards, stacked and held together with rubber bands.

He laughed, his brilliant teeth showing again.

"What's so funny?"

"Nothing, babe, nothing. It's just kinda old school. Don't you know it's all computers these days?"

"So people keep telling me, and I'm not your babe." She gestured at the cards. "They're all good, active. There's gotta be five hundred of them. I have a friend who works at the post office, been collecting them for the last three months. I said I could find a buyer."

"Like I said, we work mostly in the tens of thousands nowadays, just the numbers, no need for the actual card, 'less you want to use them to buy gas."

Suki sighed. "Never mind. I got something else big

coming up next month. I just needed a few grand to tide me over."

Dajuan nodded. "You looked like a higher class of grifter to me when you sashayed in here. I can give you five bucks a piece for the cards, though."

"Five bucks?"

"It's generous, because I want us to be friends. Maybe you need some help on this other thing you got going on?" He walked over to a red tool box on the counter and opened it, took out a stack of twenty-dollar bills and started counting them off.

"I'll keep it in mind, Dajuan, but I think I got that one covered. Like you said, it's all about computers these days. I hooked up with this real odd old pair. Married."

"Married? They like Bonnie and Clyde or something?"

"Way too boring for that, but they got the skills to get my money back."

"Wait a minute." He handed her the twenties. "Your money? I thought you were stealing someone else's cash. Someone rob you?"

"Sort of." Suki sighed dramatically to show that her life was one long struggle. "It's my father. He doesn't want to part with my inheritance. He needs some persuasion."

"Oh, my guys, you need persuasion, that's our specialty."

"I'll keep that in mind. I'm going for subtle, but if that doesn't work, I might see what you can do for muscle."

She turned toward the garage door.

"Suki?"

She looked his way again. "Yeah."

"Not my usual style, but you want to get some dinner, go somewhere?"

She smiled.

"Thanks, but no. I'll be back next week with another 500 cards. Maybe we can do something then."

His teeth shone.

"I think I'd like that."

***

Now it was two weeks later, and she was back. Dajuan looked up and smiled.

"Didn't think I'd see you again, after dinner last week."

She smiled a little smile. She seemed a bit out of sorts to him.

"Everything okay?"

They had met for dinner a week after she first came to him. Like she promised, she'd come back in with another batch of cards, just before closing time, and he bought them, then suggested dinner. He thought it had gone well, but when he invited her home afterward, she kindly but firmly rejected him. She hadn't even made an excuse, just a simple "Sorry, no."

She shook her head. "Not really. This thing with my dad, it's rough. I shouldn't have gone to dinner with you in the first place. My head's just not in it. Not your fault."

He turned his smile on. "So what can I do for you?"

"That thing we talked about. Computers vs. muscle."

"Yeah."

"It looks like this job is going to take both. Are you interested?"

"How many guys you need?"

"Five."

"How much?"

"It goes right, fifty thousand each. Interested?"

"Dinner included?"

"Yes, but only with you, the other four will need to find their own dates."

"Course, baby."

"I'm not your baby."

90

# 12

The man known as John Adams sat alone, cleaning a black and silver Browning Hi Power pistol. He didn't like guns, as a rule, but he liked to have one handy on a job, in the unlikely event that things went off the rails.

He set the gun down on the counter next to another pistol, a Ram X50. He stood from his stool and stretched, looking around the windowless room.

He was in his stronghold. The basement of a nondescript townhouse he owned on Kenmore. He rented the three apartments upstairs, but kept this space for himself, down the stairs and behind a steel reinforced door. It had metal shelving all down one wall, holding boxes filled with anything and everything one might need for a job, accumulated over the years. Wigs, uniforms, climbing equipment, scuba equipment, surveillance devices, boots, you name it. There were boxes of protein bars and energy drinks. With the small cot he could unfold and the toilet and shower in the corner, he could live locked away down here for a month if he ever had to go into hiding. Of course, if it came to that, he would prefer a quiet tropical island somewhere. His odds of ever needing a place like this were small, but he liked having it in his back pocket.

Also on the counter was a laptop, which he flipped open to check on the device Abby had planted at Grafton last week. It was running fine. He could see into most areas of their mainframe, though frankly it was all Greek to him. All he cared about was that it was undetected, which he could tell from the monitoring menu along the side. Green lights all the way down.

Adams was young enough to be part of the information revolution, but he'd missed it completely. His early years were spent in Venezuela, and then his teen years in Chicago were largely spent on the street, stealing cars.

It was the eighties, and there was a strong anti-immigrant sentiment in the air, something he's never forgotten or quite forgiven, and one of the drivers for his obsession. He can see that tide of hatred rising again, and there is big, big money behind it. In Adams's mind, you fight money with money.

A lot of terrible things happened to him during those years, things he's never even told his wife, but he learned a lot, too. Once, he found a wallet in the glove box of a car. The photo showed a twenty-year-old soldier with dark eyebrows and a shaved head. That's when he realized how easy identity theft was, and he rode that ID and those credit cards for a week before Mastercard got wise and shut it down. In those days it took a lot longer. Long enough to buy new clothes, some firearms, and a month of nonperishable food.

He learned a lot about bullies, and when to fight them and when to sidestep them. How to use their own confidence against them.

The biggest bully he encountered was a fifty-year-old man named Richards who ran a car-theft ring. He looked like Sean Connery in *The Untouchables* and blustered about loyalty and courage, but he treated his stable of young thieves as disposable. He had no qualms about putting them in harm's way.

Adams was twenty at the time, putting himself through the University of Chicago, where he enjoyed literature and drama. Even tried acting classes. The crime paid his tuition. One day, when he missed a job because of a midterm, Richards found out Adams was in school. One of the other young guys had snitched. Richards said he would make sure Adams was kicked out of school so that he would never screw up again. That was it. Adams took a tire iron and beat Richards senseless. Not to death, but close. He and a few of the others loaded him into a stolen Mercedes and left him in front of Cook County Hospital. He was taken from there directly to jail upon recovery. They never saw him again.

The other car thieves were willing to make Adams their new leader, but he didn't want anything to do with being in charge of anything. He distrusted organizations on instinct, and he wanted to finish his degree.

That was when he reached out to Eldon Shelby. Don, as he was called, was just a few years older than Adams, but had made a name for himself fencing goods. They had met when Adams found a purse full of jewelry in one of the more expensive cars he stole. At the time, he knew nothing about how to sell stolen jewelry without being caught. Don was connected, his grandfather or great uncle or something like that was a legendary mobster, which gave him many advantages when he set himself up in business. But he was also smart and fair and had a sense of justice that Adams shared.

Adams told the crew they had a new boss and gave the business to Don. In exchange, Don gave him seed money for whatever he wanted to do after he graduated, and they parted friends.

\*\*\*

Adams sighed and looked around the room. He hadn't intended to become so introspective; he didn't believe in wallowing in his own problems. Neither had he intended to be a loner, but he had trust issues. And, in his business, trust was always a problem. He tried to think of one real friend he had besides Don, and of course Abby, and came up short. Their associate Danny was a good guy, and they often hung out even when there was no job on, but he wasn't a confidante.

He thought of Abby again and sighed. This job was taking a toll, and they'd been having issues even before it began. It's one thing to know something is going to be emotionally tough in theory, and another to live through it. He thought about their daughter, and how he had hoped they would make a family, and they had, even if it was an unorthodox one. But she was thirteen when she came to them, and a short few years later she was out on her own, running her own scams. It happened in the blink of an eye.

In some ways he had hoped the family arrangement would distract Abby, who spent a lot of time trying to figure Adams out: what he was thinking about, what he wanted from life. Then she would be upset when she found it was always the same thing, like a bigger job, another payday, or a new plan. That's just how he was wired. It was a burning pain in his lungs that only eased when he felt he was making progress on his mission to save the world.

He laughed out loud in the empty basement chamber. Jesus Christo, he took himself seriously. He looked down at his black suit coat and black pants. When this was over, he was going to buy a bright orange Hawaiian shirt to wear on vacation. That would make Abby laugh, if she had any mirth left in her after next week.

He sighed, put the Browning pistol back in its case, and tucked the other gun into his belt at the small of his back. Time to get home, or his wife would start to worry.

# 13

Kirk was working his way carefully through the apartment of Mr. and Mrs. Adams. He had started with the refrigerator, because he was starving. A cursory look around the big room, while he ate a sandwich, revealed little. He didn't even know what he was looking for. He didn't want to steal anything, just wanted to know a bit more about whom he was dealing with. A little leverage, like their real names, for instance.

He looked in the daughter's room. It looked like a typical teenager's room, but what would he know? Beyoncé poster, more books than he would expect. A dresser full of clothes. No photographs.

He wandered into the master bedroom and went straight to the bathroom. Opening the medicine cabinet, he found a first aid kit. If they returned suddenly, he'd say he was changing his bandage. The bathroom was typical of the ones he'd been in that belonged to married couples. A shaving kit and deodorant, a toothbrush, and then a crap-ton of women's products. He looked at the big jar of foundation and thought again of Abby's face. Why so made up? Adult acne? Hideous burn? Giant scar? Had to be something.

He looked for medicine bottles, hoping to get a name, but there was only one bottle, and it had the name John Adams on it. The prescription was for Zyprexa, which Kirk googled on his phone. It was for bipolar disorder. Interesting. He had noticed that John would be very calm, and then suddenly quite agitated. He wondered if it was connected in some way. He wondered what would happen if someone stopped taking it or took something they thought was Zyprexa but was something else. He opened the bottle and took a picture of the pills with his phone.

For now, he would stick to the plan. John was invaluable; he needed John's expertise to make the plan work. A million dollars was just the beginning if he became a regular member of their group. That much seemed clear. And John had welcomed him and given him the opportunity. But...what if he found a way to keep the entire thirty million dollars? He wouldn't need anyone, ever again. Would he retire to a small island somewhere? He looked at himself in the mirror and smiled. What kind of man are you, Jacob Kirk? One who honors his agreements? Or one who seizes opportunity when it presents itself? He shrugged. Time would tell.

The bedroom revealed nothing interesting. They had no pictures, no paperwork, no knickknacks. Nothing. The place was a glorified Marriott.

He returned to the bathroom and gingerly removed the bandage from his forehead, tossing it into the trash can. He leaned forward and examined it under the bright vanity lights. It looked okay, the little butterfly bandages were holding it together. He probably should have gotten a few stitches, but it was closing well. He'd probably have a little scar, but that would only make him look tougher. He decided he didn't need the gauze anymore and was headed back to the kitchen for another sandwich when his cell phone rang. It was a number he didn't recognize.

"Hello?"

"Jacob, it's Suki."

That was a surprise.

"Suki?"

"Yeah."

"You all right, Abby okay?"

"Abby's not here. It's just me, but I could use your help."

"Where are you?"

"I'm at the police station."

"What?" His pulse quickened.

"I'm not under arrest," she clarified quickly.

"Well that's good. Not hurt?"

"No. Can you come get me?"

Kirk hesitated. A bit too long.

"Right. I get it, sorry."

"No, no it's fine," he said quickly. "Which station."

"The one on 63rd. You don't even have to come in, I'll meet you across the street."

"What are you doing way over there?"

"Long story, but Jacob..."

"Yeah?"

"I really didn't want to call John or Abby. I just don't think they'd understand. I didn't want a lecture."

"I get it, Suki, really, I do. I just gotta go get my car and I'll be there. Give me thirty minutes."

"Okay. Thanks, Jacob, really."

"On my way."

\*\*\*

Meanwhile, John was on a side street in Bucktown, walking leisurely along the sidewalk in his dark suit, breathing the night air. Up ahead a silver Volkswagen Beetle sat at the curb. One of the new ones. John remembered the old ones. You could start them with a screwdriver. You could almost pick them up and carry them away. This one wasn't the nicest car on the street, but he was drawn to it. He gave a quick look around for anything suspicious, then walked around to the driver's side, sliding the slim jim out of his sleeve as he went.

A quick move, and he was inside the car, setting the tool on the passenger's seat, pulling his tool kit out of the inside pocket of his coat.

Two minutes later he was cruising down Lake Shore Drive. The little car had a sunroof, so he slid it back, even though it was getting crisp in the evenings now. The fresh air woke him up and improved his mood.

It was ridiculous—and he knew it—but stealing cars was therapy for him. He'd been doing it for so long and was so good at it, it felt like home. He leaned his head back against the headrest, his thoughts wandering to just how much money they could milk out of Grafton Corp before they were discovered. Why stop at thirty million? Why not just push it until the alarm sounded and then get out, quick? They'd run the operation from the apartment, which they were planning to vacate anyway. He knew they could be out of there in twenty minutes or less. Faster than Domino's Pizza. As long as the gizmo did its job and alerted them to a trace, that would be plenty of time.

Even if they were surprised by authorities at the apartment, Adams had escape routes planned. He had backup plans for his backup plans.

And he had plans for the money, as much as they could drain. He'd never felt as free of conscience before. Grafton Corp didn't do pensions, they didn't do universities or medical savings accounts. They were the go-to company for wealthy people trying to get even wealthier. Lionel Banke's daughter would get her money straight from Lionel Banke's account. That would be just. The rest would come from the top one percent of America's top one percent. How much would it take before it even hurt them a little? One hundred million? A billion?

The problem with a score like that is they would come

looking, and they would look for a long time. Getting in and out without anyone noticing would be better, even if it meant a smaller take.

Back and forth he went in his mind, until he slowed the little round car and eased it into a parking spot on North Marine. Yes, it was best to clear the apartment after this one, leave the city, head to Europe maybe. It would be easy to disappear, take a vacation, secure in the knowledge that the millions that they stole would be put to good use, by groups they had carefully vetted. They'd have to parcel it out slowly, over several years and across dozens of organizations.

He strolled up the block toward the apartment and was about to turn toward the front entrance when something on the opposite side of the street caught his eye. It was Abby, sitting on a bench, staring up at the building. He crossed and sat quietly next to her.

She turned to look at him and laughed. "Shit, you're not even in there."

"I'm right here."

"I see you. I was just sitting here preparing myself to go in and face you in front of Jacob."

John put his forearms on his knees, looked down at his shoes. "Today was hard, I'm sorry."

"Really hard."

"*Si.* Really hard. And it's going to get worse. But we will handle it, and things will be better afterward."

"Will they?"

"I promise."

She laughed, and he turned to look at her. "You don't believe me?"

She took his hand. "Of course I believe you. You've never broken a promise to me. I just wonder what 'better' means to you, and if it's anything at all like what I think it means."

He was about to answer, though he didn't know what he was going to say, when his phone vibrated. He reached into his coat pocket and pulled it out.

"It's a text from Kirk. Wants us to meet him at the restaurant over on Broadway. It says urgent."

"Seems everything is urgent these days. On the other hand, I'm hungry."

Adams stood and held his hand out to Abby. She took it and pulled herself up and put her arms around his waist.

"I love you," he said.

"I love you, too." She pulled back and looked into his familiar face. "Let's go eat, I'm going to need my strength."

# 14

"I have to ask you again, Miss..."

Suki hesitated a moment. "Adams."

"Miss Adams. What were you doing in that part of town?" The detective was straight out of central casting. In fact, Suki would have sworn he was the guy from Blue Bloods. The son, not the mustache guy. This guy wore a crappy suit, had very badly cut brown hair, and had either forgotten to shave that morning or his beard grew ridiculously fast. Sitting opposite him, in the noise of the squad room, she checked his hand for a wedding ring. No wedding ring.

"It was my Lyft driver," she told him again. "He let me off in completely the wrong place. I didn't realize until he had already gone. I was talking to a friend on the phone. Clarice? She was the one who told me about this party? I walked right in the door, thinking everyone would be there, but it was just this crappy old warehouse." She paused and set down the icepack she had been holding against the back of her head.

The detective, whose name was Richter, started to get up. "You need another one? Gone warm?"

"No, it's fine," said Suki.

"Are you sure you don't want us to take you to the hospital?"

"No, really—"

"It would be best to check it out."

She motioned him to sit back down, and he did.

"My friend is coming to get me in about twenty minutes," she said. "If it keeps hurting, I'll have him take me to the doctor." She smiled at him. "It's just a bump."

"You're a lucky woman," he said. Was she? A woman? She could have been seventeen, or she could have been twenty-five. Either way, he was thirty-two, and a cop. Best to keep his mind on the incident.

"Well, a little luck," said Suki, "but as I said, I've taken martial arts for the last five years. I think I caught him by surprise."

"Could you give a description of any of the others?" asked Richter.

"No, not really. They were way down the other end of the warehouse. All men, I'm pretty sure. Five or six of them. White. That's when I said screw my wallet and took off."

"And where was this, exactly?"

Suki sighed. "I told you, I'm not telling. No way. I got inside there, where I thought the party was? I heard women screaming. Screaming! I turn to leave and he's standing there, blocking the door. I have no idea where he came from. I must have walked right past him when I came in; I was looking down at my phone. I turn to run, and he hits me, hard, right on the back of my head. I don't know what with—maybe his fist. I don't know. I fell down hard, seeing stars."

Richter leaned forward. She was giving more detail than the first time through, and he didn't want to miss anything.

"This guy's got a walkie-talkie," she continued. "I hear him say, 'You guys missin' any girls up there?' This guy on the other end, says, 'Nah, don't think so.' My guy says into the thing, 'I'm outside two seconds, I come back in there's a girl here.' The other guy says something I couldn't make out, about keeping the door locked, and my guy says, 'Whatever. Come down and get her.'" Suki's eyes grew wide and she clutched the edge of the desk as she remembered the scene. Richter put a hand out as if to comfort her but thought better of it.

"That's when he grabbed my purse," she continued. "I was starting to get my senses back, got up on my hands and knees, he's looking through my bag. Takes my wallet, looks at my license. I heard a noise and looked up to see more guys coming through a doorway at the far end. I kicked straight back from where I was kneeling." She picked her foot up high enough so Richter could see her heavy-duty leather boots. "I think I broke his knee cap. I don't wait, I run for the door, then I look back to maybe get my purse, but the other guys are running toward me now, and the guy on the ground, he's still got my wallet gripped in his hand. 'I'm gonna fuckin' kill you,' he spits at me, and I just run. Out the door, down the alley, onto the sidewalk where there were lots of people. I ran three or four blocks. That's when I started to feel dizzy."

"Officer French says you collapsed right next to his cruiser."

"I must have. I don't think I passed out, but things got a little hazy."

"Miss Adams, you've got to tell me exactly where this happened."

She shook her head and her long braids swung from side to side.

"No way. That guy has my wallet, my license. Got my address on it. I'm going to go live with Clarice for a week or so, then find myself a new place."

"We can protect you," said Richter.

Suki was standing now.

"Uh-uh. If I hadn't run into that police officer, I wouldn't have come here at all. No offense, you seem like a sweet guy, but you all don't seem to have a clue about the shit going down in this city. The murders, the shootings every weekend."

"That's completely different."

"Is it? I don't think so. You can't tell me there aren't cops involved in that sort of thing, with the women. Otherwise, you'd have shut it down by now."

"I'm sorry, but that's just not right." He sat back in his chair and crossed his arms.

She softened a bit. "Look, my ride's probably outside by now. I'm sure you're really a good guy, but I just don't trust the police. I'm going to lay low, not say anything."

He stood up and started to walk her toward the exit.

"Are you sure you're okay?" Richter asked her again. Suki put her hand up to the back of her head.

"Yes, I'm fine. There's not even a bump!" she said brightly.

"You're lucky. You've got my card?"

She pointed to the front pocket of her jeans. "I do."

"Please, if you change your mind, call me. You could be saving someone's life."

Suki shook his hand and then headed down the hall and out the door to where Kirk was waiting to pick her up.

Richter watched her go.

\*\*\*

Kirk looked up when John and Abby entered Grace's African Restaurant. He enjoyed the look of surprise on their faces when they saw him seated at a table for four with Suki. He waved them over, noting the hard line of John's mouth. Abby, on the other hand, took it in stride as they both sat at the table, John next to Kirk and Abby next to Suki. Boys against girls, Kirk thought, but knew that wasn't quite the way things seemed to be lining up.

"Have you ordered any food?" asked Abby, pretending there was nothing strange about the situation. Almost as if by magic the waiter appeared, a tall white guy with a wispy goatee. Kirk didn't think it likely he was from Ghana, but hey. A job's a job.

"So you know what you'd like?" the young guy asked the table.

"Fufu and chicken soup," said Abby, without hesitation.

Kirk raised his eyebrows. "That was quick!"

"We come here now and then," smiled Abby.

"I'll have the same," said John, he was looking down at his hands, folded on the table. He seemed to be avoiding eye contact with Suki.

For her part, Suki looked the menu over and said, "Yeah, sure. Me too."

Kirk shrugged. "I have no idea what any of this is, Suki picked the restaurant, but if all three of you want it, it can't be that bad." He smiled around the table, receiving only a sharp look from John. Kirk wondered if it was jealousy he was seeing on John's face.

The waiter noted their orders and retreated. The moment he was gone, John spoke.

"Ok, what's this all about, Jacob. Why are we here?"

"Actually, I think it's best if Suki tells you herself."

John and Abby both turned expectantly to the girl.

"Umm. You see, I called Kirk because I was at the police station—I knew you'd get mad, it wasn't like that. That's why I called Kirk."

"Hey," said Abby, raising both hands. "We're not your parents."

"But if we were—" John began.

"Let her tell the story," Abby said, reaching across the table and putting a hand on top of his tightly clenched fist.

So Suki did. About halfway through the story their food came, which Kirk was glad to discover was really good. Score one for Ghana.

"I don't understand, honey," said Abby, mothering despite herself. "Why were you trying to do business with the Dajuan guy anyway?"

"You've got to be careful," John said, his voice calm and, he hoped, wise. "You can't be putting yourself in dangerous situations when a big job is about to go down. We all need to lay low until Friday."

"Right, like at the aquarium."

"Different. That was something we needed for this job."

"So was this," Suki said, and made a funny motion with her eyes.

"I don't understand," said Abby.

"You know," Suki said, then paused. "Before..."

"No, honey, I don't."

Suki blew out a breath of air that somehow expressed how thick all people over the age of thirty were.

"Fine," she blurted. "Last week, when you didn't trust Jacob, I thought I had a connection to find us some guys."

Everyone started talking at once until John snapped his fingers. Remarkably, the other three hushed.

"Please," he said. "Let me go first, then everyone gets a turn." Kirk glowered but nodded. Suki folded her arms and sat back in her chair like someone who was about to get a lecture. "First," said John, turning to Kirk. "I didn't know you. I didn't trust you. I'd have been a fool to not have a backup plan if we decided not to cut you in." Kirk started to open his mouth, but then clamped it shut. It was hard to find fault in that. "Secondly," John continued, looking at Suki, "we've been over this before. You hired us, but you don't run the job. This goes well, you get two and a half million dollars. I suggest you use it to move to Europe and go to college, far away from your dad, who is definitely going to have some suspicions. But

106

if you don't want to do that, if you want to take the money and start your own criminal enterprise, go for it. Until then, please, I beg you, let me handle the details. Si?"

"Fucking *si*," growled Suki. "Just remember, I'd be burnt to a crisp right now if I listened to all your ridiculous precautions." She leaned diagonally across the table and pointed in his face. "Life's chaos, mister, you can't control every tiny detail." She sat back in her chair.

John looked across the table at Abby.

"Your turn."

"Oh, I'm good," she said, reaching for her water glass. "I think Suki just about summed up anything I had on my mind." She took a long drink. "Jacob?"

Kirk smiled.

"Look, I get it. I've been running my own gang for almost ten years now." He looked at John. "Burden of leadership and all that, but I gotta tell you, this little ship of yours seems to be floundering, John."

"It's—"

"Ah, ah, ah," said Kirk, talking over him. "My turn, remember? I'm hanging with you all week, excited to make this job work. Bigger than anything I ever done? Hell, yeah. But it has got to work, or it's—"

"It'll work—"

Kirk held up a hand to stop him. "Meanwhile, my guys are back in Ravenswood doing god knows what while I'm not there. And that's fine, I'm tired of that, but for me to let it go I need this job to work, and for this job to work you need guys. And I got guys." He looked pointedly at Suki. "No offense, Suk, but you got no experience at this at all. You oughta listen to these two and do what they say."

Suki looked up. She seemed shocked, as if she had started to believe that Kirk was actually on her side in this game, if there were sides, but of course he was just another old white guy who felt entitled. She frowned at him.

"Like I say," Kirk continued. "I got the guys. They're ready, I'm ready, and it seems to me like the plan doesn't work without us, and if it does work, we do most of the heavy lifting."

"That's absurd," said Abby, who suddenly looked more indignant than John. "We have the tech, we have the plan, we have the client."

"Yeah, yeah, yeah, I get all that," said Kirk. "And I'm good with it. I just think me and my guys deserve a bit more of the payday."

"We are not renegotiati—"

"John," said Abby quietly.

"—ing this deal. You're getting an even cut!"

"What do you want, Jacob?" Abby asked, turning to look at him.

"Abby, we already gave him—"

"Hush," said Abby. "Jacob?"

"Quarter mil for each guy," said Kirk without hesitation. He'd already thought this through. "I'm not trying to be a dick here, I appreciate what you're doing for me, but I'm planning on cutting these guys loose after, and joining up with you. They got to feel satisfied they're getting an adequate parting gift, or they could make trouble. Could even make trouble during the job."

"Is that a threat?" asked John.

"You got it all wrong, John."

The waiter appeared at his elbow. "Is there anything el—"

"Fuck off," said John, without turning to look up at him.

The waiter retreated quickly.

"Nice," said Abby, frowning across the table at him.

"Wait a minute," Suki interjected, suddenly coming

alive. "Don't be stupid. You got what, ten guys? That's more money than the whole job."

Kirk grimaced but said nothing.

"What?" Suki was furious at his silence.

"You'll have to ask these two about that," said Kirk.

Suki whirled on Abby. "What the fuck is he talking about?"

"Later," she said. "We'll talk about it later."

John Adams stood up from his chair. He took out his wallet without saying a word and dropped some bills on the table. They were all looking at him. He looked back at them, each in turn, and when he spoke his voice was soft.

"This job is good. This job is solid. This job is a career maker. And it's perfect. You have to trust me, because if you don't it won't work. The only thing that's going to derail this is us. We will defeat ourselves if we aren't careful, with all this squabbling." He turned to Kirk. "Two-hundred grand for each of your guys, and an extra five-hundred thou for you. If you trust me, and follow the plan, we can do many more jobs together after this is over. If it doesn't work exactly as I say it's going to, we don't ever have to see each other again afterward." He turned to look at Suki. "I think you should let us take you to a hotel tonight, to be safe. We need you as much as you need us, and besides, we like you and don't want to see anything happen to you. I'm going to get the car."

With that, he turned on his heel and left.

Abby looked at Suki and then at Kirk, who drummed his fingers on the table with his gaze fixed on the napkin dispenser in the middle. Finally, after most of a minute had gone by, he looked up at Abby.

"Good," he said with decisiveness. "All good. I'm good." He stood up, took his leather jacket off the back of the chair and swung it on. He looked down at Suki. "You need a lift or you good with all this?"

Suki looked at Abby then back at Kirk, who shrugged. "Really, kid, I'm fine either way."

"I'll stay," said Suki, looking at Abby.

"Right, no worries," said Kirk. "Just a little bump. This is all going to work just fine, just like John said. Call me, either of you, let me know what's next. I gotta go get my guys lined up."

He headed for the door, turning back once to look at the two of them still sitting side by side, both looking away from each other.

# 15

Levesque downed the last of her Red Bull and tossed the can in a trash barrel as she passed briskly by. It was still early in the morning, but the signs pointed to an unseasonably warm day. She could feel sweat prickling the small of her back as she strode down the sidewalk.

"Levesque," she said sharply into her phone.

"Yes, Lieutenant. This is Sergeant Griggs."

"What is it, Griggs?" A crowd of tourists were waiting for the cross signal, blocking her forward motion. Jesus, she thought, someone was always blocking her way. Didn't everyone else feel the same way she did, that there wasn't enough time in the day for everything that had to be done?

"We got the fingerprint report back from that school bus."

Levesque knifed her way through the crowd and jabbed the walk button repeatedly. What a bunch of morons.

"Great, lay it on me."

"It was clean. No prints."

The crowd around her was talking in another language. German? Hungarian? It was hard to hear what Griggs was saying.

"Did you say, 'no prints'?"

"That's right, Lieutenant."

"You mean besides the kids'."

"What kids?"

"It's a school bus, Griggs, it should be covered in kids' fingerprints."

"No, nothing. Was it maybe just cleaned?"

"Fuck!"

It was clear the group of tourists spoke at least a few words of English, because they fell silent and stared at her. Levesque glared back, and the light changed. She stayed where she was on the corner and watched them cross.

"It was cleaned all right," she told Griggs, "but not like you mean. Somebody took care to wipe it down." She sighed. "What have we got from the Shedd people. Video?"

"Well, about that. It seems that their surveillance system wasn't—"

"Working that day. Of course. Of course it wasn't. Is that all you got for me, Griggs? Because that's nothing."

"That's it."

She hung up without signing off, then turned up the sidewalk instead of crossing, her mind racing. It was unorthodox, but shit, she wasn't getting anywhere this way. She paused in the shade of a skyscraper and leaned her back against the cool cement wall, put her hand in her pantsuit pocket and pulled out a rumpled business card. She looked down at it, her phone still ready in her other hand.

What the hell did that even mean, The Levelers Co.? Who the hell did these people think they were?

She took a deep breath, ran through a plausible story in her head, then called the number.

*** 

Jacob Kirk caught himself staring out the window again, watching the heavy cloth strips dance back and forth, spreading suds across the windshield of a Honda Pilot. His thoughts had been on the same cycle for a while now:

John, Abby, Suki, money. John, Abby, Suki, money. Lionel Banke. He could see the man in his mind, running down the field, stiff-arming defenders as he went. He'd be a lot older now, but still a potential threat if things went sideways during the heist. He mused about bringing a gun, and if so which one.

The Honda moved on along the automatic treads of the car wash and was replaced by an old black Ford from the 1960s. Was that a Falcon? Galaxie? He squinted but the suds covering the car made the little silver letters impossible to read. Or maybe he needed glasses. Christ, he was getting old. He wondered who was driving such a great car, but he couldn't see in through the driver's window.

"Boss..."

Tuco's voice brought him back to earth, and he turned away from the window and back to the staff room of the car wash, where his crew sat watching him. They were all solid guys. Tough. He'd thought about hiring some women. Sometimes on a job you need a woman to make a con come off right. Other hand, it always caused trouble. He looked at Tuco, who clearly would have trouble working with a woman. The guy was distracted enough as it was.

"Right. Sorry. We've got to focus, myself included." He put one foot up on a chair and leaned forward on his knee. "This is more money than any of you have ever seen, so we want to be cool and play it straight. It's a solid plan, and so simple. Couldn't be more simple, right? Questions?"

Kevin spoke up.

"I just want to be sure I got this straight." He was a young guy, maybe twenty-two, and spent way too much time working out. Still, thought Kirk, he'd clean up well with a nice dress shirt, take out the eyebrow stud.

"What is it, Kev?"

"Well, it's like robbing an office, instead of a bank."

"Exactly."

"But there's no security guards?"

"Right."

"So, well, if it's so easy, why isn't everyone doing it?"

Kirk laughed.

"You know what, Kev? That was my exact reaction when I heard it explained to me. Why are we killing ourselves breaking into rich people's houses, risking alarms, dogs, gun-toting housewives, when all of their big money is kept by these so-called financial institutions?"

There was a murmur from a few of the others.

"I'll tell you why," Kirk continued. "It's because the money is invisible. You need a computer expert to get at it. They've made it too hard for everyday criminals. It's like fixing cars." He gestured behind him to the window that looked over the car wash bay. "Washing 'em's easy, but look under the hood these days? You need a computer to even figure out what's wrong. The system is rigged. Who makes all the money in this economy? The people who already have money, that's who. And who scores all the easy white-collar crime? White-collar criminals, computer hackers, that's who."

He stood up straight and crossed his arms over his chest, pleased with his little speech.

"You really gonna retire after this?" asked Nelson.

Kirk scratched his beard.

"Yeah, think so. You should think about it too. Two hundred grand, you can buy a condo. Get a real job. Go to night school and become a computer whiz so you can get in on the real money."

"Yeah, maybe," said Nelson, clearly unconvinced. "I was thinking more of what we got going here. Who's gonna run it with you gone?"

Kirk shook his head to show his sad acknowledgement of Nelson's shortcomings.

"You want to be a dinosaur, Nelly, fine. You've been with me longest. You give me your two hundred, you can have the car wash, everything in the basement, all my contacts. I'm checking out." Or moving up, he thought, but did not say out loud.

"I'll think about that," said Nelson.

"You do that, but do it quick. We got less than two days to go."

***

Danny checked to make sure the car was dry, then leaned against it and pulled out his phone.

"Hey John, it's Danny.... Yeah, just did it. It's right where he said it was. I caught a glimpse of him talking to a bunch of guys in some kind of meeting room.... No, no chance he saw me and if he did, so what? Just getting my car washed.... Yeah, I think he's legit.... You could maybe go in at night and plant a bug.... Right, I hadn't thought of that, anyway, you know all that stuff better than me anyway."

He turned his face up to the warm sun as he listened to John Adams once again make him an offer that was hard to refuse. Nevertheless, refuse it he did. He'd had a lucky life and he knew when to quit.

"No problem, John. Glad I could help. Let me know if you need anything else, and take care of yourself.... You, too."

He hung up the phone and slid it back into his pocket.

He loved the guy, but he was going to get himself killed one of these days.

# 16

"Well, I like your choice of meeting places, better than John's." Kirk bit into a Giordano's slice with gusto. "I'll say that."

He and Suki were sitting on a bench in a little garden just outside the entrance to Navy Pier. It was a warm afternoon, and Suki wore a purple tank top and big, pink-framed sunglasses. Kirk was in his regular uniform of jeans and T-shirt.

"I mean honestly," he continued, despite his mouth being full of pizza, "Wizard of Fucking Oz Park."

Suki wasn't eating. She sat leaning back, her elbows on the back of the bench, her head slowly moving side to side as she scanned the many pedestrians passing by. Kirk noticed.

"Don't worry," he said. "John is off meeting his equipment guru, the guy with the thingamajig. I'm sure Abby's with him."

"I wouldn't be so sure about that," said Suki, still scanning the crowds.

"What's that supposed to mean?" Kirk asked. Now he was looking around, too. "What are we doing here, anyway?"

"I trust you, Jacob."

He turned his attention back to her, but she was inscrutable behind the mirrored glasses. He smiled. This could be it, but he had to play it subtle. He had a pretty good idea this might happen, after the scene at the restaurant. Still, he would play it cool, see if her plan was a good one, then he'd decide. Let it seem like her idea.

"You should trust me," he said smoothly. "It's in everyone's interest that this job goes well; I've already made arrangements for what I plan to do afterward."

She pulled her iPhone out of her pocket, started to hand it to him, then pulled back.

"I'm trusting you," she said again.

"Absolutely," he said, his face serious, his slice of pizza set to the side.

She handed him the phone, which was open to the recording app.

"Just listen to this."

His eyebrows went up.

"I recorded it last night," she continued. "On the way to the hotel, after you had left."

Without ceremony, Kirk pushed the play button and held the phone to his ear.

\*\*\*

"—idea what that means, do you?" John's voice was loud.

"John, just—"

"No, this—"

"Calm down!"

"I'm calm," John shouted. "I'm calm," he said again, softly.

"This is not about us," said Abby, also calming her voice. "It's about this job."

"My job," said Suki, her voice closer to the phone and louder than the other two.

"It's not always that simple," said John. "We have a lot of balls up in the air, not just this job."

"What's that supposed to mean?" asked Suki.

"We've got someone out there who's after us," said John, "for a previous job."

"And the cops," added Abby.

117

"Cops?"

"We're taking care of that too," said Abby, matter-of-factly.

"I don't care about any of that. Those are your problems, I just want to make sure they don't fuck up the plan. I want to make sure this goes right. It's my job, I brought it to you."

"That doesn't mean you can interfere," said John. Kirk heard the muffled sound of a car horn.

"It means exactly that!" Suki's voice got angry. "Listen to me. I. Am. Your. Boss. Not your daughter."

"I don't—"

"We don't—"

"Of course you do," Suki insisted. "You, you think you've got all the answers, and my input is laughable. And you, you want to be all friends and let's go shopping and shit. I don't know why your daughter took off, but it's not hard to guess."

"I don't think—"

"I think she's right," said John.

There was a dead silence in the car.

"You what?" Abby's voice had a dangerous edge.

"We aren't treating her like a regular client, because she's a kid."

"I'm NOT a kid."

"Sorry, you know what I mean. Abby, we have to leave our own troubles out of this."

"Our troubles?"

"Yes."

"Our troubles??"

"You know what I mean."

"No, John, I don't. I know what your troubles are. I live with them every goddamn day."

~~There was a rustle and then the sound of open air.~~

"Get back in the car, where are you going?"

118

"I've had it."

"Abby, c'mon." Cars behind them were starting to honk. "The job is in two days."

"Fuck the job!"

A car door slammed. More horns honked, and Kirk could hear the rev of an engine, followed by a few seconds of silence.

"Don't worry," said Adams. "She'll be back, she'll be fine."

"You say so," said Suki. "All I know is you better work your shit out quick."

"It'll be fine. Here's the hotel, do you want me to go in wi—"

"Nah, just drop me off out front."

"You have enough cash?"

"I'm fine."

"Because you shouldn't use a credit card—"

"No shit, Sherlock."

There was the sound of a car door opening, then closing, then the recording ended.

*\*\**

Kirk handed the phone back, trying to keep the concerned look off his face. He looked around the small grassy area, at the hundreds of people walking to and from Navy Pier, even mid-morning on a Thursday.

"Well," he said at last. "That's a bit fucked up."

"No shit. What do we do about it?"

He turned his gaze back to her. He liked her style. Obviously, she was way too young for him, and hell, he'd be rich soon, he could court whomever he wanted. Better to keep his mind on the job.

"We do nothing."

"What? Did you hear that?"

119

"We don't actually need Abby for the job," said Kirk calmly. "We need John, and we need you, and we need the gadget. Don't panic. They are the best in Chicago at this, maybe the best in the whole country. No matter how screwed up they are, they'll deliver."

"What if they don't?"

"You mean, could we do it ourselves?"

"If we have me, and we have the gadget, would we need John?"

Kirk considered the idea. "The plan is pretty foolproof. If we had to, we could do it without them. But it's going to be fine."

"Right," said Suki.

"Let me think about it," said Kirk. "It might be a good idea to have a backup plan, just in case they really do fall apart. Time's short, but maybe I can make something work." He looked over at her again. "Why are you coming to me? Do I look like someone who double crosses his team?"

Suki stood up.

"No, Jacob. I trust you because I can tell that you want it more than they do. They're completely wrapped up in each other, and their own baggage. This job falls apart, they just move on to something else. But this is a big step for you and me. I need to make sure this gets done, and I trust you to do it more than I trust them."

She turned and walked off across the grass. Kirk watched her ass as she went, but his mind was spinning on other things. This could work, he thought to himself. Definitely. He gazed after her until she turned the corner around some greenery and disappeared.

It's not like he hadn't considered it. Of course he had. Suki would still get her three million. He'd take all the rest, and that would be just the beginning. He looked down at his watch. He had a friend in London who could set up some private banking channels for him. He knew if he did it, the money would have to move fast, just like he'd have to move fast to get out of the country once the job was done.

A swatch of bright color caught his eye, and he looked back over at the sidewalk near the entrance to Navy Pier.

A small person, dressed as a pirate, stood stock still, holding a bunch of brightly colored balloons that floated above their head. It was a woman, and despite the eyepatch and big red beard, he was pretty sure it was Abby Adams. She was about thirty yards away, but just close enough that Kirk could see her wink at him.

Then, she let go of the balloons and they shot skyward. He only glanced up at them for a second, but when he looked down the pirate had disappeared completely into the crowd.

What the fuck was that about? thought Kirk. Had she watched the entire conversation with Suki? Where was John?

Maybe he was better off just sticking to the plan. He got up quickly and walked off in the opposite direction, leaving behind his empty pizza box. Best not to underestimate them, he thought. He headed off to make some arrangements, both financial and otherwise.

"Play your tricks before the game even starts," he said to himself. "Or some shit like that."

# 17

The man known as John Adams dropped cautiously over the outer wall, checked that all the sight lines were clear, then moved quietly through the window opening and into the remnants of St. Stephen Church in Hyde Park. There was no longer any window, just a broken frame. He wasn't used to breaking into buildings during the day. He made sure that the ridiculous Cubs cap he was wearing was pulled down far enough to shade his face, and that the collar of his black windbreaker was up.

An accomplished thief, he moved quietly down the dark hallway, even though the floor was littered with plaster and broken glass, not to mention discarded trash. The place gave him an eerie feeling, and he was glad he had his pistol tucked into the back of his belt, even though he had no expectation of needing it.

He slowed as the hallway ended in an enormous open space. Light poured in from a round skylight set at the apex of an astounding dome. The nave was completely empty: no pews, no altar. Just piles of trash.

Adams stood still, staring around the space. Suddenly, a bird chirped close by, making him jump. He looked around until a second chirp allowed him to zero in on the sound. There, on the other side of the space, a man stood leaning against the far wall. He chirped once more for good measure, and then stepped toward Adams.

"Don?" Adams asked.

"*Mi buen amigo*," said the familiar voice of Eldon Shelby. Adams relaxed. There was enough light streaming down to see clearly, but the man in front of him looked nothing like his old friend. His hair was dyed a yellowish white, he wore different glasses—wire instead of black plastic—and he was wearing what looked like a scientist's lab coat. It had dark, disturbing stains on the front of it.

They met in the middle of the space and clasped hands.

"Do I dare ask?" Adams said, gesturing at the outfit.

"Got another job going on today. Just had to step out to give you this." He reached into his oversized pocket and took out what looked like a regular iPhone. He handed it to Don. "It works exactly as I described."

Adams put the phone in his pocket without looking at it. If Don said it did what it was supposed to, it would.

Don had a look of professional concern.

"Did the other thing not work?"

"Oh, yes, it's fine," Adams said, holding up the phone. "This is just insurance."

"Where's your lovely wife?" Don asked.

"She's otherwise occupied, at the moment." He looked up at the skylight.

"Everything all right?"

"It'll be fine," Adams assured him, and then changed the subject. "This place is something else."

"Yes, some say it's haunted, because every deal to redevelop it over the last twenty years has fallen through. I'm thinking of having a Halloween party here."

"How's the old man?" Adams asked.

"Sharp as the proverbial tack. Wonders why he hasn't seen you lately."

"Spinning a lot of plates at the moment. Maybe the most complex one I've ever done."

"Well, you know I'm always around if you need me."

Adams hesitated for a moment. "Actually..."

"What is it?"

"It's Nick I might need. I think it might be time to

disappear for a while and resurface as someone else."

Don's younger brother Nick was an accomplished fine-art painter, and also exceptionally skilled at forging false documents.

"What is it?" asked Don, searching his friend's face, sensing something else.

"A police lieutenant, Levesque, had one of our business cards."

Don's fake blond eyebrows raised above the frames of his glasses.

"I know," said Adams, as if Don had spoken. "We're very careful who we give those out to, or who we allow to give them out on our behalf."

"You know I take that responsibility very seriously," Don said. "I'll take a close look back through and see if I can find any weak spots."

"Thank you, but we've already figured it out. I originally thought it might be from the diamond job."

Don squinted, thinking. "I can't see that; I'm pretty sure that was tight."

"Don't worry about it, it's fine. But this job tomorrow is going to send shock waves when it comes to light. So," Adams shrugged, "probably a good time for a reset anyway. Might go visit the home country for a while. Or Europe."

"Both of you?" asked Don.

"Of course," said Adams with his usual confident voice. "I've got to get going now." He patted his pocket. "Thanks for this, and good luck on the whatever," he added, motioning again toward the strange lab coat.

"Thanks, I'm having a great time."

They parted, each heading toward a different exit. With his hand on the graffitied door, Don turned back.

"Amigo?"

"*Si.*"

"Be careful, okay?"

Adams just laughed and made his way back down the dark hallway.

***

The man and the woman stood side by side in the shop, looking at a bookcase full of titles about writing. They were both in disguise. She wore a red beard and an eyepatch. He wore a rubber pigeon mask that covered his entire face. Every few seconds he made a cooing sound.

Madeleine Levesque approached them cautiously. She hesitated, looking around the shop for another pair that could possibly be the people she was supposed to meet. No luck. Everyone else was in groupings of the wrong number of people or the wrong mix of gender. She took a deep breath and stepped forward.

"Excuse me," she began. The two strange figures turned toward her.

"Yes?" said the pirate. She had an ugly scar that started at her cheekbone, ran beneath her fake beard, and disappeared down the collar of her white pirate blouse.

"I'm looking for a title called Detective Clifton Woolridge's Never Fail..." she stopped, wringing her hands and searching her memory.

"System for..." prompted the woman.

"That's right. System for Detecting and Outwitting all Classes of Grifters and Swindlers." She showed a moment of annoyance, but then smiled and seemed visibly relieved to have made it through the recitation.

"I don't believe they sell that here," said the pirate, "but let's take a look over in this alcove."

She led Levesque over to a quiet area with racks of disguises, and no other customers.

"Madeleine?" she asked.

"Of course I am," said Levesque, brusquely. She was starting to get angry. This whole thing was ridiculous. These people couldn't possibly be who she had been told they were. This place, a spy shop? In Wicker Park? Just the idea of it was preposterous. But she played along. "I mean, yes. I'm pleased to meet you, but you must forgive me if this all seems, I don't know, a bit odd."

Adams smiled behind her beard. She loved this place. Run by 826CHI, the goofy spy store was actually a nonprofit offering writing classes for underserved teenagers in the city. She and John were generous donors.

"Arrgh," she said, in her best pirate voice. "Ye can't be too careful these days, ya know." She was a very unconvincing pirate.

Levesque turned to the pigeon, who twitched his head to the side and cooed.

"And are you Mr. Adams?" she asked.

"No," said the woman. "This is one of my associates. I suppose you might call him a henchman."

The pigeon gave a stiff bow.

"Okaay," said Levesque, drawing out the "a" sound. She was in danger of losing her objectivity. Were they just fucking with her? "Can we turn to the business at hand?"

"Certainly," said Adams. "How can we help you?"

"Well, it's complicated." She leaned in so that she could lower her voice. "My husband has been missing for a week."

"Mrs. Levesque, we tend to specialize in items, not people."

"Yes, but he disappeared with many of my personal items. Very expensive personal items."

"It would have to be a considerable amount for us to be interested."

"I assure you, it is. But, more importantly, I want to make sure that there are some punitive steps taken." She

126

let her words hang ominously in the air.

Adams pulled her beard down so Levesque could see her concerned face. "You mean..."

"Yes, I want him killed. And I'll pay more than you could possibly be asking."

Adams's eyes widened. "I don't know, Maddy, we could be asking an awful lot. It really depends whether you want to do this a la carte, or prix fixe."

"What?"

"Are you looking for a package deal?"

"You think I'm kidding?" Levesque snarled. "You think this is some kind of joke?"

"No, I don't think it's a joke. I think there's been a mistake. How did you hear about us?"

Levesque was fuming now. She reached into her blazer pocket and pulled out a heavy cream business card. Stuck it in Adams face.

"Who gave you that?" Abby Adams asked, her face serious. She reached into her own pocket, causing Levesque to take a quick step back in alarm, but when her hand came out it was holding a business card of her own. "Because," said Adams, handing her the card. "I think there's been some mistake. We do children's parties."

Levesque looked at the card. It had a cartoon of a pirate holding balloons on it and said "Revelers Co." in a purple papyrus font.

"Revelers, Levelers," Adams continued. "Clearly a mistake. We are not remotely who you think we are."

"I think," said Levesque, her voice was still low, but she was spitting venom. "I think, I know, that you're responsible for the Drake diamond robbery, and at least half a dozen other felonies."

Adams laughed, and the pigeon cooed again.

"Oh dear, Lieutenant Levesque, I think you're mistaken."

At the mention of her rank, Levesque knew, of course, dammit, that she'd been made. She didn't know when or how, she only knew she wanted to grab this little woman by the throat and strangle her.

"You think," she began, "you're so superior. I think I'll just arrest you right here and take you downtown and see what we can find out."

"On what charge, officer?" Adams smiled, her beard still hanging around her neck.

"On whatever charge I want."

"That's the way you're going to play it? Throw out the rule book?"

"I'll do whatever it takes," Levesque said.

"Well," said Adams. "I'm afraid you can't arrest us." She pulled her beard back up into position.

"And why the hell not?"

The pigeon man turned his beaked head to the side and pointed toward the front of the store.

Levesque looked. There was nothing there.

Abby took one step forward and punched Levesque square in the face as she turned back. Her head whipped backward, and she dropped to the hardwood floor like someone had cut her strings.

Abby shook her hand out as everyone else in the store turned to stare. At the far end of the space she could see through the window to the sidewalk, where several men in dark suits were jumping out of an unmarked police car that was illegally parked at the curb.

"C'mon," said the little pirate, dragging the pigeon man through a nearby door and into the back part of the building where the writing classrooms were. They hurried through to the back hallway, turning right into a small office instead of rushing out into the back alley. The office had a single desk, occupied by a middle-aged bearded man working on a spreadsheet.

"Hey," he said, but Adams held her finger to her lips as the pigeon pushed past them to slide open the one window.

"Shh," Adams said, and winked her eye that wasn't patched. "Secret agent stuff," she whispered and, giving a good pirate laugh, she slid through the window and down to the parking lot on the side of the building, where the pigeon had already started their getaway car.

# 18

Kirk stood on the curb, waiting in a dark grey suit which he had to admit looked rather good on him. He had to suck in his gut a little bit; he was spending too much time lately talking and eating. He made a mental note to get back on a regular exercise regimen.

He pulled his phone out of his pocket and checked the time. It was exactly 4pm. When he looked up again a little silver Volkswagen Beetle was pulling up in front of him, Abby at the wheel, wearing a long, shiny black wig, dark sunglasses, and a frown.

He opened the passenger's door and ducked into the car, turning to see John folded into the back seat, wearing his standard black suit and white shirt, no tie. Thinking back, Kirk didn't think he had seen John wearing anything else since the first day he met him.

Kirk pulled on his seat belt as the car accelerated away from the curb and into traffic.

"This suit okay?" he asked.

Abby didn't look away from the road, but John leaned forward from behind her to get a look.

"That looks great, Jacob."

"Okay for tomorrow, too?"

"Perfect."

"Right, then. So what's this all about?" He'd been practicing a British accent all afternoon, and only narrowly avoided using it now. Maybe he would use it during the job, just to throw police off the trail. He'd gotten pretty good at it by watching Lock Stock and Two Smoking Barrels a few times last weekend.

John reached diagonally between the seats and handed him a large green cell phone. "Turn it on," he said by way of explanation.

Kirk did and was greeted with a normal passcode screen. He typed in 7531, the number that, during the job briefing, John had said would unlock the device. It did. He'd been listening intently, just in case he ended up having to do the job on his own.

"See the app called Banke Account?"

"Yeah, clever." He pushed the button and a new screen popped up.

"It's asking you for destination numbers, press 3."

Kirk did and three input slots popped up, the first said Suki, the second said Adams, and the third had a flashing cursor.

"Type your routing and account number in there," said Adams. "You've got one, right?"

Kirk shifted in his seat and pulled out his wallet, removed a small slip of paper and copied the number into the phone.

"You might want to memorize that," said Abby, without turning her head. Her voice was flat and devoid of emotion.

Kirk ignored her. When he typed in the number and pushed enter, a screen popped up asking him to assign a nickname to the number. He typed in "Kirk" and hit enter. Now all three lines were full.

"What now?"

"Hit the blue button."

A new window popped up labeled "Source."

"At this point," said John, "if you were a regular user of this app, you would type in the account number that you wanted to transfer the money from, it would ask you the amount and how you wanted to split it between the three destination accounts."

"But we're not doing that," Kirk surmised.

"No," said John, a grin in his voice. "Type in 'f=1357'."

Kirk did it and hit enter. Nothing happened except a small triple beep and the "Source" box disappeared.

"What happened?"

"That code starts the Wi-Fi hack and the extraction algorithm."

"English, please."

"The device will break into the nearest banking system and identify the accounts most suitable for draining."

"I like the sound of that. What makes them most suitable?"

"Well, balance size, for one, of course. But also likelihood of illegal activity, based on several criteria. We're looking for money that belongs to people that are going to be slow to go to the cops."

Kirk whistled.

"As well as time until the theft is noticed. Depending on the size of the institution, and the amount you pull, their internal alarms can trip anywhere between instantaneously and forty-eight hours. We want a solid twenty-four hours to be out of the country before they have figured out exactly what is wrong with their system."

Kirk shut the phone off and handed it back toward Adams.

"No, Jacob, you keep it. You're going to need it."

"Why am I going to need it?"

John leaned forward and pointed through the windshield.

"Are you crazy?" said Kirk.

"He's crazy," Abby confirmed.

They had pulled up and parked in front of a little coffee shop on the corner of Clark and Foster. What Adams was pointing to was across the street. The North Side Federal Savings Bank.

"We have to test it, Abby. We can't go into Grafton tomorrow and not know if it works. We won't get a second chance, we can't just walk away."

"He's right about that much," Kirk agreed. "With the plan as it stands, they're going to know that we're robbing them."

"Just not how or how much."

"Yeah," said Abby. "I get it. I get how it works. It's just an unacceptable risk, this close to the most important job of our career. I trust our supplier; he's never let us down before."

"We've never done anything this big before, love. Trust, but verify."

She could hear the grin in his voice and turned all the way around in her seat until she could see him. "You think this is fun, don't you?"

"Little bit, yeah." John ran his hand through his hair, pointed again at the bank. "Look at the place, love. It's so nickel and dime. It will be like old times."

"I don't want old times," said Abby. "I want new times."

"All right, all right," said Kirk, before an argument could erupt. He was warming to the idea. He'd only robbed one real bank, and the thought now of the adrenaline rush sent a prickling joy down the back of his neck. Theft by computer was so abstract. More lucrative, by far, but less fun. "Let's do it. But shouldn't we have disguises?"

John pointed up the street, to where a Vintech security truck was parked.

"Actually, their security cameras have all been on the fritz since about three pm."

"Jesus, man, you really do think of everything."

"Let's hope so," said John.

"Yes," agreed Abby, her tone dark. "Let's hope so."

***

Even with the security cameras off, they put on some basic disguises in case anything went wrong. John reached over the back seat and into the little hatchback of the car, pulled out a black briefcase, opened it, and started handing out wigs: long and red for Abby, blond for John, and a trim black one for Jacob.

Kirk folded down the sun visor to look at himself in the little mirror. The simple wig transformed him completely. It had been a decade or more since he'd had hair. He had first shaved it because it was tough-guy chic; he'd wanted to look like Jason Statham. Then when he decided to grow it back, he realized his hair had receded so far at the temples that he looked, well, old. So he'd gone back to shaving his head. He ran his hand over his black beard, which he'd only had for a year or two. The wig was a perfect match. John really did think of everything.

Abby reached into her bag and pulled out a makeup compact and handed it to Jacob.

"I look too pale?"

"The tattoo," she said without a smile.

Kirk dabbed some of the makeup over the snake tattoo on his neck, careful not to get it on his dress shirt. He checked the effect in the mirror. It would do.

He turned to Abby and studied her heavily made-up face.

"Abby, I've been meaning to ask you..."

"Save it," she said in a clipped voice, taking the compact back and putting it in her bag. She had added glasses to her disguise, tinted green. They weren't sunglasses, that might have seemed suspicious, but they would make her very hard to recognize later, based on details given by a teller or a customer.

134

Not that it would come to that, thought Kirk. If this worked the way it was supposed to, no one would ever know anything was amiss until they were long gone. And if it didn't work, that meant the job tomorrow would be a no-go, and Kirk would be hard pressed not to kill the both of them for wasting his time.

They climbed out of the little car and crossed the street. Kirk looked over at John, who smiled back. His blond wig didn't change his appearance much, but suddenly his posture and his entire walk was different. Kirk noticed even his face was set in a different expression than he normally wore. Not for the first time, Kirk wondered what the story was here. How does a guy become a professional con man? How does he become a con man who wants to give all his money away? How the hell does he find a woman who feels exactly the same way? He shifted his glance to Abby. Her spine was so ramrod straight with tension that he thought it might explode out of her back. She was seething behind her calm mask. Maybe they didn't feel the exact same way. Maybe she was ready to keep the money for herself and settle down on a little island paradise.

Which immediately made him think of sex. He shook his head. Abby was good-looking, sure, in an exotic way that wasn't his usual taste. And, she was older. So was he, sure, but one of the great things about money, in his opinion, was that it tended to erase a lot of age difference when it came to sex. He wasn't looking for a teenager—hell no, experience counted too—but maybe someone twenty-nine or thirty.

They entered the bank and split up, Abby and John going to a side counter that held deposit slips and pens, Kirk heading across the lobby to the first customer service desk he came to. He carried the briefcase, now empty, in his left hand and the green phone was in the inside pocket of his suit jacket. In the far corner, near a potted plant, stood a security guard, female, middle-aged, and bored.

An attractive woman rose from her chair as Kirk approached. She was exactly the type of woman he had been thinking about a moment ago: around thirty, long, light-brown hair, high cheekbones, a business suit that was tailored perhaps a bit too tight for this little bank. Clearly, she had ambition to go somewhere.

"Can I help you?"

"Yes, I hope so," said Kirk, using his British accent. He lowered himself into one of the chairs on the other side of her desk, and she sat back down. "I'm just getting started looking for a flat to buy and I wanted to talk about mortgages. Seems a good idea to get that ball rolling before I actually go out and commit to anything."

"Of course, Mr..."

"Windsor, Jacob Windsor."

"Mr. Windsor. I'm Kelly Parsons, you can call me Kelly. Do you have an account here?"

"I'm sorry, I don't. I suppose that would be the first step?"

"That, and some basic financial information." She stood again. "I'm just going to go and grab a few forms that we'll need."

"No worries," said Kirk, smiling as he drew the green phone from his inside pocket. "I have to return a few text messages."

He watched the contours of her skirt as she walked away, then looked down at the phone. Turning it on with his thumb, all he had to do was push the blue button. They had already agreed on $20,000 for Kirk, and the same for John and Abby. It was a small amount, but it was a small bank and they didn't want to attract any attention. Everything had already been entered, he just had to press start, which he did. The phone gave a small vibration and then the screen went blank except for a little hourglass icon that appeared in the middle, digital white sand slowly descending.

He put the phone back in his pocket and turned to look around the lobby. There were a few people in line for the tellers, and the tall black security guard by the door. He could see a gun on her hip. He knew there was no need to be nervous, but he wished he had brought his own gun. Even just in the empty briefcase. He would have felt more confident.

On the far side of the lobby he could see John and Abby. They were still standing next to the little supply counter, but they seemed to be having a heated conversation. He couldn't hear them from this far away, but Abby kept pointing in John's face, and John kept raising both hands in a sign of surrender, or simply trying to calm her, Kirk couldn't tell.

"Here we are," said Kelly, returning to the desk and startling Kirk. When he jumped, startled, she followed his gaze and frowned. "Hmm, they don't seem to be having a good day."

"I bet you see all kinds of people in here," said Kirk.

"You would not believe."

She nodded knowingly as she sat.

"Good stories to tell the family around the dinner table," Kirk said.

She looked up sharply; the question was obviously meant to determine her marital status. Could she not get through one damn day without some guy...

"Fuck you!"

The red-haired woman's shout echoed across the lobby.

Kelly turned to look. The man was clutching her by the left upper arm and putting his face close to hers.

137

Kirk pivoted as well.

"Oh, shit," he said out loud, making to rise and then catching himself.

Abby brought her left hand up and onto John's forearm, grasping and twisting until she broke his grip, bringing her right fist around at the same time to connect with his jaw. John raised his own fist but then hesitated, at which point the security guard stepped forward and yelled.

"Hey! Stop!"

With a flick of her right hand, Abby slapped a cup full of bright green pens off the supply counter and straight at the head of the security guard. She tried to duck, but the cup hit her shoulder, pens flying everywhere.

"Jesus, lady, what the fuck?"

The guard reached for her walkie-talkie. As she drew it from its holder on her belt, Abby stepped forward and kicked hard at her, catching her hand and sending the walkie-talkie flying across the lobby where it shattered against a marble pillar. A customer screamed.

The guard reached for her gun, but John stepped between the two women, one hand stretched out toward each of them.

"Whoa, woah, woah," he said. "Let's just calm down."

"Fuck that shit," said the security guard, drawing her gun anyway. John brought his outstretched hand down hard on her wrist, grabbing and twisting the gun out of her hand in one fluid motion. The guard looked up to find the barrel pointed straight at her.

"I said calm down," John repeated, and the guard raised both of her hands in surrender.

Kirk looked back at Kelly, who was staring open-mouthed at the scene. She was in shock, but surely someone somewhere was pushing a silent alarm. What the hell were those two playing at? He couldn't figure the angle, but he was sure there must be one. There always was.

In his pocket the phone vibrated twice in quick succession. Transfer complete. Right then.

"I'm out of here," he said to Kelly, rising and heading for the door.

John glanced quickly over at Kirk, who was almost to the door. A few of the customers gasped at the audacity of the bearded man, trying to leave in the middle of a robbery. Was that guy crazy? What would the gunman do?

He did nothing. John kept the gun trained on the guard as Kirk walked out the front door. Suddenly something hit John lightly in the back of the head and clattered to the ground. It was another pen. He walked in an arc, still facing the guard, until he had rotated enough to see Abby.

"What was that for?"

She picked another pen off the counter and threw it at him, but it missed and skittered across the floor. John used his free hand to rub his jaw, which still ached from when she had punched him. Abby just glared at him.

\*\*\*

Outside, Kirk sat in the driver's seat of the Beetle. He looked down at the wires protruding from the steering column. He had watched how John started the car and was ready to make a quick getaway. He lowered the window to better listen for sirens. He figured there was about a minute, tops, before cruisers started to roll up.

The front door of the bank opened, and Abby came out, turning left without looking toward him and heading up the sidewalk, taking off her jacket as she went to reveal a bright yellow turtleneck underneath. At the first corner, she removed her wig and wrapped them in the jacket, turned right around the corner of the building, and was gone.

When she disappeared from sight, Kirk looked back to the bank to see that he had missed John's exit. He recognized his back as he walked along the sidewalk in the opposite direction of his wife.

Just then, the sirens began. Whatever had just happened, it was time to go. Was the whole plan a bust now? He didn't know. He thought about the $20,000 now in his bank account. It should have felt good but would be a sorry consolation prize if the job at Grafton Corp. fell through. On the other hand, he had the green phone and Suki had the fingerprint.

The sirens were growing louder. He put the car in drive and pulled away along Clark. He fished his cell phone out of his pocket and made a call. He was going to need some backup.

***

Would it kill them to hang a picture, thought Levesque, or a goddam plant? She felt like she was in an interrogation room, not a conference room. And then Richter entered, and she almost laughed. The guy was right out of central casting. Had she stepped into a time warp instead of a police station? Was it 1978?

Frickin' Chicago. What the force needed was more women. What was it, twenty percent? Something like that. What it really needed was more women bosses. Behind Richter was a very fit man with close-trimmed blond hair and striking blue eyes. Now, we were getting somewhere. He can't possibly work in this shit hole. She stood.

"Lieutenant Levesque? I'm Alex Richter." He turned to

the dishy guy. "This is Agent Caleb Carter, with the FBI. He's looking into drugs and some trafficking of girls from Canada."

Carter had a strong handshake and looked her straight in the eye.

"Pleasure," he said, and she agreed. She didn't know what trafficking had to do with any of her cases, but really, who cared?

They sat around the small table and Richter handed her a folder, which she opened.

"These are two of the most likely trafficking suspects in that area. We've been keeping tabs on them, but haven't been able to make any solid connections."

There were sheets on two men: a Dajuan Freeman and a Jacob Kirk. She stared.

"By your face," said Richter, "I see you recognize someone."

Levesque nodded, putting a finger on the picture of Kirk. This was weird. She turned to Carter.

"Are you after the couple?"

His face was blank.

"I don't know what you mean. I'm after people moving girls from Canada into the states. Likely a whole gang, not a couple. What are you talking about?"

"High end robberies," said Levesque, leaning back in her chair and tapping her index finger repeatedly on the picture of Jacob Kirk. "Man and a woman. No violence. Hell, no guns even. Con artists, like Thomas Fucking Crown. It's almost like they're laughing at me—I mean the force, laughing at the force."

"Would they be involved in something like human trafficking?" asked Richter.

Levesque gave it a moment's thought, but the image of the stupid little pirate wouldn't leave her head.

"No, I don't see that. But," she leaned forward and

pushed Kirk's picture toward Richter, "I saw this guy with them yesterday at the aquarium. You think he's your guy?"

"We don't know, really," said Carter. "We just know these two run gangs in a part of the city where we've had some leads. My money's on Freeman, and even that's just a guess. We've really just started working on it. There are other suspects, but we were hoping one of these two could lead us to more information. They're obviously involved in illegal activity, so they would be likely to roll on someone bigger to avoid prison."

"We can't move on them without probable cause," said Richter. "We have what may be a witness, but she's hesitant to speak. She does, we'll be able to take that to a judge."

Levesque had a confused expression. "I don't get it."

"What?" asked Richter.

"I don't get what I have to do with this. I work robbery, mostly miles from here."

"Right," said Richter. "Well, there was a little bit of an error, it seems. You're working on something for a friend of Councilor Sposato, Menard."

Levesque rolled her eyes.

"Jesus, yes, that woman won't let me be. Some stupid ring, like she couldn't buy a hundred more. Meanwhile, these two I'm chasing tricked the manager of The Drake into giving them a box full of diamonds worth a cool three million."

Richter just sat and watched her fume. He could've sat there all day, frankly. She wasn't bad looking, and he bet she could beat half the squad in a fist fight. He liked that.

"Wait a minute," said Levesque, sputtering to a stop. "What error?"

"I don't know how it happened." Richter said. "Doesn't make any sense, but somehow one of the files from the

Menard job ended up being delivered here instead of to you. A clerk came across it yesterday."

"What file?" Levesque stood up in her impatience, causing both Richter and Carter to push back slightly in their chairs.

"There was a print logged as being found at your crime scene, for some reason it wasn't in the report you got earlier this summer. It came here instead."

"And you just found it yesterday?"

Richter edged his chair a few more inches back. Carter tried not to smile; he was very glad he had nothing to do with Lieutenant Levesque.

"As I said—"

"Who's print is it?" she shouted.

Richter looked down at the photo on the table.

"Jacob Kirk."

Levesque, for an uncharacteristic moment, was speechless. Her mouth opened, then closed. When she opened it again, she was no longer shouting. Her voice was slow and quiet, almost a whisper.

"What. The. Fuck?"

# 19

The man sat at Arturo's Tacos, in the last booth, so that he could have his back to the wall. Old habit. He was eating tacos and drinking out of a silver flask he had brought in with him. The management didn't seem to mind, even though the place had its own bar. It was that kind of place, long and skinny with booths and windows down one side, bar down the other. There was a big neon clock that showed that it was 2:30 am.

*\*\*\**

Halfway down the room at another booth sat a man named Nelson, with his friend Tuco. This was meant to be a solo job, but Nelson didn't care. It was a snoozer, and he and Tuco had business to work out about a shipment that was due on the weekend. Fuck it, it's called multitasking.

Still, it was a job, and Nelson took it seriously enough to glance, every few minutes, at the guy in the last booth. Not so often that anyone would notice, of course. He wasn't a fucking novice. He took a look now, while Tuco was shoving half a burrito into his hole.

The guy looked like he had a bit of cash. Nice black suit, nice white shirt. But he also looked like he'd been stepped on, worn out. You could see it in the eyes. Haggard's the word he wanted. Stubble, hair slightly disheveled. Drinking out of a goddamn flask, for fuck's sake.

Actually, Nelson thought that was pretty badass.

Bringing your own flask to a bar, like maybe you only drank the finest whiskey, something they'd never serve in Arturo's. Maybe he'd get himself one like that. He couldn't think of anyone else in the gang who had anything like that at all. It'd be his trademark.

"I said what about Spitzer!" Tuco was talking through his mouth full of food. Nelson hadn't been listening, so now Tuco repeated himself. Tuco had a shaved head, like most of them did, but he also had this crazy handlebar mustache—his trademark—which currently had smears of guacamole in it.

"Spitzer's too pappy," said Nelson, speaking out of the side of his mouth, his eyes still on Adams in the far booth. "I don't trust him to handle that cargo. And wipe your fucking mouth. It's disgusting." He slid his untouched paper napkin across the table to Tuco, who had already used his beyond recovery.

Nelson had a shaved head too, and no facial hair. Gotta shave your head every morning, you might as well do your face while you're at it. He wore silver-rimmed glasses, and a dark-blue, button-down shirt that, unlike Tuco's shirt, was free of salsa stains. He kept himself looking nice. He didn't have any visible tattoos, and hell, half of the stock brokers on Wacker had shaved heads these days. With his glasses, which he needed all the time now, he could fit in with more polite company. That ability could come in handy for some jobs.

He looked over again at the sad man with the awesome flask. He watched him tip it up, and then all the way up, clearly draining the last drops. The guy was a mess. Maybe lost his job, maybe lost his wife. Nelson didn't know and didn't care, he was just supposed to keep tabs on him, which he had been doing for almost seven hours now. He'd pretty much had no choice but to call Tuco and have him meet on the job, 'cause it didn't seem like this job was ever going to end. Did the guy have a house? Did he ever go to sleep? He looked like he was ready to nod off right there in the booth. In fact, his head had just started to tip back when a rowdy crew of college kids came through the door, talking at full volume.

"What about Squid? Or Pete?" Tuco was still on task, you had to give him that. If he just wasn't such a fucking slob.

***

Adams sat at his table, screwing the cap onto the empty flask. He placed it into his inside jacket pocket, fumbling with imprecision, grunting with annoyance. He looked down at the remains on his plate and considered another plate of tacos, rubbed a hand over his belly and decided against it.

Life wasn't getting any easier. He had set high goals for himself, and he didn't regret it, but sometimes he wished things would just be simple. Maybe he should go out and steal a few cars, like he did the night before. Blow off some pressure.

He closed his eyes and leaned his head back, aware that he was being watched. Stealing cars in the middle of the night, before the biggest job of his career, what was he thinking? Is this what it meant to move up the ladder, that you almost immediately wish for a simpler life? A vision swept into his mind unbidden of wildfires in California, earthquakes in Mexico City, long lines of migrants fleeing warlords and lawless cartels. He had reasons for his greed. He was greedy on behalf of those who were so beaten down they didn't even know how to be greedy. This job was a quantum jump toward his goals. Nothing else mattered.

His thoughts were interrupted by a cacophony of brash

young voices. He opened his eyes and raised his head to see four young men come in, talking at full volume. College students, drunk on a Thursday night. They seemed oversized to him: rugged, tall, white.

They would be perfect.

He staggered slowly to his feet and made his way down the narrow aisle. When he reached the table where the two thugs sat, he swayed hard to the side and put his hand on their table for support, then moved on.

The four guys were still standing, talking, waiting for a table. Adams approached them, stepped to the side as if to go around, but then tripped and fell directly into one of them, a black-haired guy with a DePaul sweatshirt. The guy grabbed Adams by the shoulder to steady him.

"*No me toques!*" Adams shouted in his face. The guy raised his hands in mock surrender, but one of his buddies, a thick set guy with a buzz cut, stepped forward and poked Adams in the chest.

"Chill out, little man," he said.

"*Vete al diablo.*" Adams pushed at the guy with both hands, but the bruiser barely budged. On the contrary, he stepped forward and pushed Adams, hard, sending him staggering backward down the aisle. Adams swung his arm out wildly, as if to catch himself, and connected hard with the back of Nelson's head, where he sat facing Tuco. He leaned into it, thrusting Nelson's head down fast and hard so that his face bounced off the Formica table.

"Jesus Christ!" Nelson roared as he leapt up, one hand grabbing his nose, which was already spurting blood. The force of his reaction sent Adams reeling back toward the college kids, who all suddenly turned pale. He heard shouts from behind the counter and turned around to see that Nelson had drawn a gun.

He turned back toward the front door and sprinted for it, just as the college boys were crouching down in terror, desperate to get out of the line of fire. Adams didn't look back, he was confident that the man would not shoot him in the back. Pretty confident. He took two more steps and leapt into the air, using both hands on the back of the DePaul boy to vault over him. He landed on his feet and kept his momentum going, crashing into the door and pushing it open without stopping. He flew out onto Armitage and then quickly jogged down North Wilmont Ave, the adrenalin and the cool night air clearing his head.

He took a quick look back. Nobody.

He slowed to a walk and pulled his phone from his jacket pocket. No messages, voice or text. He noticed the time. Shit. Tomorrow was going to come early.

# 20

"More headroom in this little thing than I imagined."

"I guess."

Kirk was sitting up straight in the driver's seat of the little silver Beetle, his comment a pretense for turning until he was directly facing Suki, who sat slumped in the passenger's seat. The damn gear shift and console divider was keeping him from making any serious move toward her. Probably for the best; he had told himself he wasn't going to get involved. Too young, too many strings attached. He'd have his pick of women when he was rich. Still, he could use a bit of sex to calm himself down before the big event.

It was just before dawn on Friday, but he'd been up most of the night taking care of little details to make sure everything went as planned. It still felt like the middle of the night to him. He reached a hand out, despite himself, and laid it on Suki's left shoulder.

Suki reached over with her right hand, took his by the wrist, and removed it from her shoulder, letting it drop back on his side of the car.

"That's not what I'm here for, Jacob."

He was disappointed. He'd be lying if he said he wasn't, but he was glad that she didn't seem mad about it. Suki was all business.

"Right, sorry. Just excited by the job." He ran his hand bashfully over his shaved skull. "I wouldn't normally admit that to anyone, but you—"

"Save it," said Suki, holding up her hand.

"Right, sorry."

"Look, Jacob, I'd like to get this wrapped up so that we know what's what. I just need to know about John."

"What about him?" Kirk seemed confused.

"You and him: Are you friends?" The sun was not quite up, but the sky had lightened considerably, and he could see her face clearly. Her left eyebrow raised slightly when she asked the question.

"He's okay, he and Abby did me a real favor, but we aren't friends. Why?"

"You aren't business partners?"

"Maybe, and a week ago I might have wanted that, but now I'm not sure."

"Not sure how?"

"He seems unstable, and this thing with him and Abby, it just seems like they are going to blow up any minute. Surely you're thinking the same thing."

She nodded. "Do you think we should call the job off?"

He took a long slow breath. "I've been debating all week whether to trust them or bail out. Now I'm thinking there might be another choice."

"Meaning what?"

"I'll tell you something else I shouldn't tell you," he said. His voice was thick with pride.

"What's that?"

"I had him followed yesterday, by one of my guys."

Suki gasped. It was the first excitement he had seen in her, and it warmed him to elaborate.

"That's right. He had this crazy idea to pull a little job to make sure all the tech worked, but soon as we started, he and Abby got into it, right in the middle of this little bank."

"Wait, wait, wait. You were robbing a bank?"

"I know, it's—"

"Fucking crazy! What if you all got caught? My job is today!"

150

"I know. He had a point, though, about a test run, so I went along." Kirk shook his head in disbelief. "She punched him in the face, right in the middle of the bank."

"What?"

"That got the security guard's attention, I can tell you. Then she picked a fight with the guard."

"Abby? I thought you said it was John you were worried about."

"Well honestly, I don't know what the hell to think. She's definitely got some anger issues, but he just lets it all roll over him. He acts like Mr. I've Got Everything Under Control when he clearly doesn't. Which is worse than her going mental. We don't need her, really, so I don't care what she does."

"But you had him followed?"

"Right." He looked at her with a serious face. "I've been doing this a long time, Suki, since I was a lot younger than you are now. Don't roll your eyes! I was protecting myself with my fists when I was twelve years old." He sat back in his seat and looked out the window at the lake. "This guy, the way he acts. So much confidence. I mean, I have to say I admire it. But..."

"But what?" Now it was Suki who was leaning toward him. He could feel her move closer, but he kept looking out the window. He could play fucking hard to get, too.

"Well, all his talk about planning, and being one step ahead. Maybe he's up to something. Maybe he's got another plan that includes cutting me out."

"He'd never do that," said Suki, her voice serious. "If there's one thing about this guy, he's honorable. It's one of the things that drives me crazy about him. And you said you owe him. Doesn't that bother you?"

"'Course it does, but you have to look out for yourself, that's the golden rule. And hey, maybe you're right and he's a saint, but I don't trust anyone, and I'm definitely right about one thing."

"What's that?"

"I'm right that he's losing his shit. He can't keep his wife in line—"

"Hey, now."

"I didn't mean it like that. Honest. I just meant she's on his team, they're working on this together, and it seems like he's the man with the plan. He should be running the show, but instead he's running after her all the time like a little puppy."

"She's kind of magnetic."

"Ya, I get the whole mysterious Asian thing, I guess, but what's with the make-up?"

"Don't know."

"Kind of strange, plus..."

"What?"

"Nothing." He looked out the window, thinking to himself with some amusement that he really didn't spend that much time talking to women. Too much time hanging in a warehouse with a bunch of uneducated jamokes. That's one thing he'd learned from John, just in this short time. You could hang with a higher class of people and be the better for it. Better for your career as well. Being in a gang in Chicago, even if you were the top dog, was not a promising career path. This job really was going to change his life. It was going to change everything.

"She's just not my type," he said at last, turning to look at Suki with a wolfish grin that left no doubt in her mind what his type was. She leaned away again, slouching against the passenger door.

"So what happened?"

"I dunno, I think my mother and father really screwed me up as far as romance goes."

"I mean the tail you set up."

"Oh, right," he said, his face coloring. "After they fight, he stomps off down the sidewalk. Walks for hours, goes to a bar and sits by himself drinking gin and tonics, then staggers to an all-night taco place. Keeps pulling his phone out and looking at it, like he's waiting for her to kiss and make up. Pathetic. He pulls a flask out of his jacket and starts drinking at the table, for chrissake."

"Well that's not good."

"It gets worse. He gets up to leave and ends up getting in a fight with a bunch of college kids."

"Oh my god, did they beat the shit out of him?"

"Oddly, no, he managed to waltz out of there without a scratch, the lucky bastard, and my guy lost him after that, but I assume he went home. I'm supposed to pick him up..." he glanced at the car dashboard clock. "...in about three hours."

Suki looked at him seriously. "Thank you for telling me, it makes what I'm going to propose easier."

"You want to cut him out, right? I couldn't tell when we talked before how serious to take it."

"Oh, I'm serious, all right, but it's worse than that."

It was Kirk's turn to look concerned. "What do you mean?"

"Well, I've been making plans, too."

"To cut out Adams?"

"And," she said sheepishly.

"What do you mean?"

"Well, when it seemed like you and Adams were tight, and you didn't immediately say yes when we talked in the park, I started on a plan to cut you all out."

Kirk nearly snarled like a dog, but somehow held it in, forcing it into a smile instead.

"That's not very sportsmanlike."

"Oh, come on, Jacob. You and I both know Adams is planning to take way more than three million dollars. He told me himself that the device will only do one job this big. Once Grafton Corp. figures out how they were hacked, they'll up their defense, and so will every other big bank in the states. Probably the world; they're all global. You all were going to go big. Very big would be my guess."

"Look, I wouldn't normally consider double crossing a partner..."

"Oh, save it." Suki opened the glove box, rummaged around until she was sure there was nothing interesting in there. "You got any mints? Or gum?"

Kirk shook his head.

"I don't really care," Suki said. "I'm not a kid. And I want to take more than three mil, too. So I planned to cut you out."

"But now you're telling me."

"Now I'm telling you."

"Because."

"He trusts you."

"And you need a crew."

"Actually, no."

"No?"

"No, I have a crew ready to go. Serious guys. But..."

"But what?"

"It's getting a little heavier than I wanted. The guy who runs them, he wants a bit more from me than I'm willing to give."

"I bet."

Suki rolled her eyes at his smirk.

"Look, Jacob. It'll be easier with your crew, it's what John expects. I've held back the last thing they need, so they can't do the job without me."

"The fingerprint."

"Exactly. Mr. Lionel Banke's fingerprint, to get past the secure door to the inner offices. The Wi-Fi hack has to be within fifty feet of the servers to work. It can't be done from outside the building."

"But why hire John and Abby in the first place if you're just going to cut them out?"

"I needed John's brain to figure out how to make it work, and his access to technology. At first I thought I could just go in there with a gun and force Banke or one of the other executives to transfer the money. I was stupid. Banke would know it was me. John and Abby convinced me it was better to do the job in a way that left no trace until we were long gone." She grinned at him. "And, honestly, I didn't realize I had a taste for it until I got involved."

"You like running around with the criminal type, huh?"

"I like being the criminal type. I've toed the line so far and got shit-all for it. Junkie mother, screwed by my dad."

Jacob smirked.

"Figuratively, I mean. Get your mind out of the gutter. How do you even get through the day?"

"It can be difficult," he admitted. "Which reminds me: How can I be sure you're not going to cut me out? Seeing as you don't show all that much loyalty to your partners."

"I'm going to give you the fingerprint before I get out of this car."

"The plan calls for you to give it to Abby. Won't they be suspicious?"

"By the time she asks for it, you'll already be in the building. It'll be too late."

Kirk smiled. "How do you know I'm not going to screw you? Figuratively."

"Because, Jacob Vaclav Kirk, I have your social security number, your driver's license, and a copy of your fingerprints from the Chicago Police Department."

His smile faded.

"How the fuck..."

"I got it from Abby. What?" she shrugged. "I said John trusted you, I didn't say she did. And to be fair, she only had it for security, in case you decided to do something stupid. Now, I have it and she doesn't." It was her turn to give a wolfish grin.

"How do you know she doesn't have a copy of it?"

"It came by courier, when I was at their apartment one day. Old school, printouts in a folder."

"Can't she just get another copy?"

"Maybe, but by then I'm guessing you'll be in another country. Whereas, if you fuck with me and I don't see my share of the money, say, twenty million dollars, in my bank account before you leave The Rookery building then I'll have my detective friend waiting for you, wherever you go. You'll never get out of the country, unless you happen to have a fake passport, or can get one before the end of the day today."

"Jesus, you're fucking diabolical."

"Thank you."

"What detective friend?"

"Oh, everyone should have one," Suki said nonchalantly, her dark skin glowing in the sunlight now streaming into the car. It was fully morning.

"You think of everything."

"It's a gift."

"And what about this other tough guy? What's he going to do when he finds out you no longer need his services? How much did you promise him?"

"He'll be fine, and if he's not..."

"Your detective friend."

"Everyone should have one."

Suki reached down between her feet and pulled up her oversized handbag. She rummaged for a minute before bringing out an eyeglasses case. She opened it and removed what looked like a flat piece of silly putty. In the slanting dawn sunshine, Kirk could easily see the whirling pattern of raised ridges on it.

"That's pretty cool. How'd you get it done?"

"John had it made. He has a friend who's really good at this kind of thing. I made him give it to me as security that he wouldn't try to do the job without me."

Kirk snorted.

"What makes you think he didn't just make another one for himself? It's exactly the kind of thing John would do."

Suki replaced the fingerprint in the case and snapped it shut, then handed it to Kirk.

"It doesn't matter if he has one or not, because you and I have a deal now, and he's never going to see the inside of Grafton Corp. today, is he?"

Kirk sat in stunned admiration. This girl was a piece of work.

"Jacob," she said, pulling his attention back to her. "This is your last chance. You can walk away completely. You can do the job with John, or you can do the job with me. What's it going to be? Do we have a deal?"

"Yes, yes we do." He held his hand out toward her, but instead of shaking it she just opened the passenger's door and climbed out of the car, the door swinging shut behind her.

Kirk watched her go.

***

Suki gave the middle finger to a guy who whistled at her as she walked past. Shit, it was six-thirty in the morning. Who thinks it's cool to whistle at a girl, like she's going to turn around and say thank you? Come over and ask you for a date? Who thinks that's going to happen at six friggin' thirty in the morning? Seriously, men are such assholes.

She kept walking, glad for her leather jacket as the fall morning was brisk. She reached into the right-hand pocket and pulled out her phone. With her left hand she slid two fingers into the tight back pocket of her jeans and pulled out a business card, typed the number into her phone with her right thumb, and pushed the button. She put the card back into her pocket while she waited for the call to go through.

\*\*\*

Abby was up early, at a coffee shop three blocks west of their apartment. She sat in the window with her laptop, brushing stray strands of her long, black wig behind her ear. It was hot and annoying. She shouldn't have worn it, but she liked to be especially careful on the day of a job.

She logged into the app that let her monitor what was happening on the Grafton Corp. server. She was unhappy, but she was a professional. She just had to get through today and then she would take a break, see how John behaved when it was all over, see how they would move on afterward. Figure out when enough was enough, if it ever was.

Everything looked good on the computer. Green lights everywhere, not a hint of anything wrong. She pushed a series of buttons that would start a program remotely. She glanced at the time, then decided to have another coffee. She would wait until John left the apartment before she began her next job for the day, her next task of the rigorously detailed plan. It was all she could do.

\*\*\*

Detective Alex Richter had just returned to his desk with a fresh cup of coffee when his cell phone rang. He took a long drink before setting the mug on the edge of his desk. The precinct coffee was actually pretty good now that they had one of those machines with the little single serve plastic containers. Curig or whatever it was. Bad for the environment, he knew that. But what can you do? He sat in his chair and brought the phone to his ear.

"Hello?"

"Hi, Detective Richter?"

"Yes, who's this?"

"This is Suki...Adams."

"Okay, Ms. Adams."

"You helped me a few weeks back, about a warehouse on—"

"Right, right!" An image leapt into his mind. Big eyes, gorgeous skin. Young. "What can I do for you?" He pulled his chair up to the desk and began searching his computer for the relevant file.

"Well, I've been thinking more about it. How you said I should tell you where it happened."

"You absolutely should. Absolutely."

"I've been staying with my friend, afraid to go home."

"Clarice."

"What's that?"

"Your friend, Clarice, you mentioned her."

"Wow, you've got a great memory!"

"Thanks," he said, scanning the file for more information. "And have you changed your mind?"

"Well. I'd kind of like to go back home and get some of my stuff."

"We can arrange an escort if that would help."

"Hmm, maybe. What happens if I tell you the address?"

"Well, the report you gave makes me think that it's

likely that the group you encountered are involved in human trafficking. I would call an associate of mine, Agent Carter, who works for the FBI, and they would get permission from a judge to enter the grounds and see what they find there."

"And I wouldn't have to be there? No one would have to know it was me?"

"I think I can arrange that. I have your statement here already, that should be enough."

"When would you do it?"

"Right away. I've already spoken about this with Agent Carter, after I talked with you. He had some suspicions about who you may have encountered, but sadly he has a lot of leads when it comes to trafficking. The problem just keeps getting worse. It's a Friday, so we'd probably try to do it right away, so we don't have to wait over the weekend."

"You mean right now? You can do that?"

Richter pulled his shoulders back a bit.

"We are here to help the city, Suki. We want to take these guys down. I'm guessing Carter could mobilize within the hour."

"That's amazing."

"What's the address, Ms. Adams?"

There was hesitation on the other end of the line.

"Ms. Adams, Suki, what's the address?"

She told him and he wrote it down, once again picturing the young woman who had sat at his desk. This time in his mind she was crying, and he reached out and took her hand.

"We will get them, I promise. Can I call you later to let you know the outcome?"

"Yes, I'd like to know. You can call me on this number."

"Got it. I gotta go now and get this rolling. You made

the right choice."

"Thank you. It means a lot for you to say that."

*****

Suki hung up the phone and crossed the street toward the Osmium coffee bar. They'd be open by now, and she really needed some breakfast. She entered, ordered an espresso and a muffin to go, then made her way to the bathroom.

She splashed cold water on her face and looked at herself in the mirror above the sink. It was going to be a long, interesting day.

After drying her hands, she reached into her pocket to pull out the phone she had just used. She glanced around the bathroom to make sure she was alone, tossed the phone into the trash can, then went back out into the coffee shop to pick up her order and head back outside.

# 22

Kirk knocked on the door to the apartment again, louder this time, then stood back waiting. It was 9:15 for Chrissakes.

He took a deep breath to calm himself. Three hours from now, this would all be over. High noon. Funny.

The door swung open.

"Jesus, you look like shit."

"Thanks," said John, leaving the door open and walking back into the interior of the apartment. "Coffee?" he called over his shoulder.

"Not sure we have time," Kirk answered, shutting the door behind him and following Adams into the kitchen area. "You were supposed to meet me downstairs fifteen minutes ago. We've got to get all the way over to North California in about ten minutes."

"Okay, okay."

Adams poured coffee into a travel mug and grabbed his black suit coat off the back of a chair. He walked past Kirk toward the door. He was unshaven and his hair was wild. There were noticeable bags under his eyes.

"What the hell were you doing last night?" Kirk asked. "You look like death."

"Nothing, nothing. Just didn't sleep well." He headed for the door.

"Abby come home?"

Adams stopped, still facing the door. Kirk watched as his shoulders tensed and then slowly relaxed.

"*Si*, of course," Adams said, turning back to smile at Kirk. "Everything is just fine." He motioned with his arm that Kirk should precede him out of the apartment, which he did, and they went down the four flights of stairs to the street, where Kirk had illegally parked his red BMW. It was about ten years old, but in great shape. Adams climbed into the passenger's seat as Kirk walked around to the other side.

"You like it?" he asked Adams as he got behind the wheel. He had purposely picked something that was fast but elegant, and not overly showy. He could be subtle, too, when he wanted to.

"Fantastic," said Adams as the car pulled into traffic. "What did you do with the little Beetle?"

"It's at the car wash getting new plates and the starter fixed."

"The carwash?"

Kirk downshifted and passed a car, but then had to stop almost immediately; morning traffic was still congested.

"Shouldn't all these fuckers be at work by now?" Kirk asked with exasperation.

"Big city. Lots of people."

"Thank you, Zen Master Flash."

"Carwash?" Adams asked again.

"Yeah, I told you, before, I think. I run my business out of a carwash. I mean, it's also a car wash, but my office is there, and my guys work the sprayers when we don't have anything else going on."

"You should become a money launderer," grinned Adams.

"Yes, you are right. I've never heard that joke before."

"No?" asked Adams, turning to look at Kirk. "Oh, you're kidding. I see. Sorry."

Kirk turned from Lake Shore onto Montrose, frustrated that it was only one lane in each direction.

Adams looked out the window.

"This is a nice neighborhood."

"Yeah, it's not like your place, but it's a big step up from where I grew up."

Adams pointed at a taqueria.

"They any good?"

"Honestly, John, I wouldn't know good Mexican food from bad. It all tastes pretty decent to me."

"Fair enough. When we get to your place, it's going to be okay that I lead the rundown?"

"Absolutely. I've prepped my team well. They know that you're the man with the plan."

"Once inside, you'll be the point man. You'll be calling all the shots while I'm in the office with Banke."

"Yeah, no worries. Just don't forget to put some cash in my account."

"I won't. I'll make sure you get what you deserve."

"That sounds more ominous than I'm sure you meant it to sound," said Kirk with a laugh as he put his blinker on and waited to turn left onto North California Ave.

Adams was looking at the beautiful park out the left-hand side of the car as the traffic cleared and Kirk made the turn.

"Fuck!" shouted Kirk, bringing the car to a screeching halt.

Adams whipped his head back toward the front to see the street ahead full of police cars and black SUVs.

"*Jesus Christo!*" he gasped, as Kirk threw the BMW into reverse and began to back up. Adams noticed that several of the men on the sidewalk outside saw them and began to point. Some were in police uniform, others wore black windbreakers that said FBI on the back in big yellow letters.

The car jerked to a halt again and Adams looked back to see that two big SUVs had blocked the end of the street behind them.

"Fuckity, fuck, fuck!" growled Kirk as he threw the car into first and wrenched the wheel hard to the left, crossing oncoming traffic and jumping the curb onto a cement walkway. He swerved around some kind of stone obelisk and continued down the pedestrian path toward a brick and cement building.

Adams looked back. One of the SUVs was still behind them, the other seemed to have hit one of the trees lining the walkway.

"They're coming!" Adams warned.

Kirk swerved around the building and onto a round green field, heading straight across toward the other side.

"River!" Adams shouted.

"I see it, I see it. Left or right?"

"Left, go left, back to Montrose."

They turned left and shot between tennis courts and the river, exiting back out onto Montrose and turning right to cross the river.

"Take your next available right," advised Adams, turning again to look behind them. The SUV had not yet emerged onto the street.

Kirk turned right and then slowed down. This neighborhood was row after row of triple-deckers with detached garages. He turned left onto an identical street and slowed until he found an open garage, pulled the BMW into it and killed the engine.

The two men jumped out without a word, Kirk reaching up and grabbing the strap that pulled the garage door down as they exited. It rolled shut with a screech, and they made their way on foot between two houses and onto the next street. He doubted he'd ever see the car again, but he had other things to worry about at the moment.

"What now?" asked Kirk, despite himself. This was his turf, damn it, but he'd never seen anything like that show of police force—and the feds! He turned to Adams for direction.

"There."

Adams pointed to the end of the street where a tiny auto dealer sat, about twenty cars on the lot. He crossed the street and approached from the side, stepping off the sidewalk and to the closest car, which was also the furthest one from the door of the dealership. It was a charcoal gray Toyota Corolla. Perfect, thought Adams, the world's most nondescript car. Adams motioned Kirk to the passenger side as he slipped behind the wheel. He checked above the visor for keys as Kirk got in and closed the door.

"No luck," said Adams, pulling his pick set from his inside pocket. "Going to have to do it the old-fashioned way."

"Well, do it quick," said Kirk, who was keeping an eye on the front of the building.

The words were barely out of his mouth when the car engine turned over. He turned to see Adams grinning as the car slowly pulled onto the street and turned left onto Western Ave, away from the dealership.

*** 

Adams was seething.

"I just, I can't..." He threw his arms up in the air, speechless.

They had continued all the way down Montrose until they got to the beach and the bird sanctuary, then left the car in the parking lot there. They walked along the wide top of the retaining wall, the lake on one side, sandy beach on the other. People were windsurfing even this late in the season.

Adams thought about pushing Kirk off the wall and

into the lake. Maybe this whole plan wasn't worth it. He could do the Grafton heist without Kirk, if he wanted to. He was swinging for the fences, and he was liable to strike out. Which was a stupid metaphor; Adams didn't even like baseball.

"I have no idea what's going on," said Kirk, "but I've got to get out of sight. I have to assume they have my picture." He had wanted to go to Adams's apartment, but John had said no, the apartment was in the process of being cleaned out; Abby would have to start over if they went in and touched anything.

"You're fine here," Adams reassured him. "Look around." It was windy and desolate out on the point. "Keep walking; it calms the mind."

"You don't seem very calm."

"I haven't shot you in the head yet, so I think that counts as calm."

"Try it."

"Now," Adams said, and began walking again, "is not the time for bravado. I have put up with you questioning me every step of the way. I've put up with Abby doubting me, which makes you and Suki doubt me. But having one person in complete control is what makes these jobs come off without a hitch. And right now, you have fucked up my plan."

"I didn't do anything!"

"You keep saying that. Yet..."

"I don't know."

"Has anyone contacted you?"

Kirk pulled his phone out for the twentieth time.

"Still no."

"Can you reach anyone?"

"I don't dare try. My guys are trained not to use autodial, or contacts. Our phones don't keep a record of calls sent or received. FBI'll have to use their tech guys to get inside and trace any calls. It'll take them days."

"Well, that's clever at least."

"Unless I call them." Kirk felt the knot in his back muscles tightening further.

"Or one of them gives you up."

"That could happen. I'll admit it. They're good guys for the most part, but there's always someone willing to stick the knife in, isn't there?"

Adams gave him a look, but Kirk was gazing out across the water.

"Yes, there is."

Kirk stopped walking again and turned toward Adams.

"They were all there. That's why no one has called. They were all there together waiting for us to go over the plan. Any of them call now, there'll be an FBI agent sitting next to them listening in."

"I've already thought of that. It means you're screwed. One of them was a rat."

"A rat? Is this a gangster movie?"

"No," Adams growled. "It's a massive fuck-up. Was it the home invasion you did up in Northfield, or was it the Bank of America job you pulled in June?"

"How do you know about that?"

"I know everything," Adams said in a flat voice.

"Oh fuck off, John. I've had about enough of the holier-than-thou from you."

"You wanted to move up, but you weren't ready. You hit a bank, you left some kind of trace."

Kirk poked him in the chest with his index finger.

"That job was solid."

"Well, now this one isn't. We can't do this without a crew."

"Is that what you're worried about? The FBI is after me. You can just go find a crew and do this job next week. I've got to get the fuck out of town."

168

"I can't do it next week. I've got to get out of town too."

"Mr. Allen?"

Adams looked down at his feet.

"Jesus, John, there you go again. I'm a fuck-up, you say, but you've got the same problem. I don't want to leave town without that money."

"Neither do I. Of course I don't, but what alternative do we have? There's no way to do it without the Mary Lou on the third floor. If it doesn't look like a robbery, it'll look like a robbery, if you know what I mean. We have to have at least five guys."

Kirk snapped his fingers.

"I have an idea where to get a crew."

"Let me be clearer: We need five guys that we know and can trust."

"Suki knows a crew."

"Suki?" Adams stood staring at Kirk in astonishment, the wind off the lake ruffling his hair.

"Yeah, she—"

"Suki?!"

"Yea—"

Adams turned and stalked down the walkway, back the way they had come, toward the bird sanctuary. Kirk ran to catch up.

"C'mon John. Just listen."

Kirk thought Adams would explode, but he just stood there and ran his hand slowly over his face, using his thumb and forefinger to squeeze the bridge of his nose.

"This is why I don't have a team," he said, almost to himself, his hand falling back to his side. "Suki has a plan, you have a plan. Suki wants in on the job, you want a bigger cut. No wonder Abby is so pissed all the time; she's seen how many ways this can go wrong."

"All due respect, man, Abby's pissed because you don't hear a thing she says."

Adams opened his mouth to respond, then stopped. Shook his head.

"Maybe. Who knows. Whatever." He sighed and looked straight at Kirk. "Why does Suki know a crew, and what was she going to do with it?"

Kirk took a deep breath to settle his nerves. A lot had happened in a short time, but maybe there was still a way to make it work.

"I'm not sure, John, but I think she doesn't trust us." He held up a hand to stop any interruption. "She thinks we're going to take all the money and cut her out."

"We've got a deal in place."

"Yeah, the fingerprint, she told me. Did you have more than one made?"

"What do you mean?"

"You know what I mean. You told her she had the only one, that she could trust you because you couldn't do the job without it."

"So?"

"So did you make more than one? Simple question."

Adams didn't say yes or no, he just stood there with his eyes on Kirk.

"Well," said Kirk. "And you think it's strange she doesn't trust you."

"Have you met these guys she's talking about?"

"No, but we really don't need them to do much, and if they muck it up and get arrested, that doesn't really interfere with our plan, after a certain point."

Adams thought about it, then smiled. "After a certain point, you're right. In fact, it would cover our tracks even more, as long as they think we're just there for the bearer bonds. But can we depend on them to get that far?"

It was Kirk's turn to smile. "Their leader's under Suki's thumb. What do you think?"

"I think they'll do whatever Suki says."

170

"She already knows you're after more than three million."

"I told her as much, that night after she was at the police station. Now she has a chance to earn a bigger share."

"I hope she sees it that way."

Adams pulled out his phone and checked the time.

"There's no way we can pull this together by noon. I'll call Abby, then I'll call Banke and see if I can change my appointment to three. You call Suki and see if she can get that crew together by two o'clock. We'll all meet and go over it, but..."

"But what," asked Kirk.

"I don't like the way that meeting goes, I pull the plug—and you back me up on it. We walk away. Deal?"

"Deal."

# 22

All the hair on the back of Dajuan's neck stood up. He had a Spidey sense, especially for hot girls. Sure enough, there she was, coming around the corner of a Ford Explorer that his man Jackie was changing the plugs on. Dajuan straightened up from the motorcycle he was working on and looked for a rag to wipe his hands.

"Suki."

"Dajuan."

"It's awesome to see you, baby. What's up?"

"I'm not your baby."

"Course not, course not. My bad. Just something I say. You are my well-respected, fine-looking female acquaintance."

"And would-be employer."

Dajuan cocked his head in surprise. "Is that so?"

"Is there somewhere we can do this in private?"

"Of course, ba—I mean, right this way." He made a motion to catch Jackie's eye and then pointed toward a door at the back of the garage. Jackie gave a big smile and a thumbs up, which made Suki roll her eyes. Nevertheless, she followed Dajuan across the shop floor and through the door, which he held open for her with a flourish.

They entered a cluttered office with a desk and chair, a flat-screen television on one wall, and shelves full of old Chilton manuals. Dajuan crossed the little room and entered a tiny bathroom.

"Make yourself at home," he called back over his shoulder as he began washing his hands. He checked himself in the mirror, then looked around for something clean to dry his hands on, struck out, and wiped them on his mostly clean cargo pants. He turned his smile up to eleven and stepped back into the office.

"Suki," he grinned at her.

"Dajuan." She was sitting on the edge of his desk, one leg dangling, her black leather jacket unzipped. All the little gold studs on it were shining in the sunlight streaming in through the little window in the back wall.

"I was just thinking about some lunch. Would you like to go get something?"

"Too much work to do. I've got a big job that has to happen today. I'm looking for help. Your help."

Dajuan raised his pointer finger and made a lazy circle, indicating that Suki should stand up and turn around.

"Tell you what," she said. "I'll tell you the job. You nod your head yes or no, and if you say yes, I'll prove to you that I'm not wearing a wire. Deal?"

"Deal."

***

Twenty minutes later, Suki had finished her meeting with Dajuan. She zipped her jacket up and turned to look at him. He was a good-looking guy. Working in a garage must be a decent workout, because he had a great body.

She'd managed to conclude the transaction without going as far as she'd thought might be necessary. He seemed to enjoy the little peek-a-boo show she put on and was willing to wait until after the job for the chance at something more. Who knows, if he was telling the truth about not being involved in trafficking, then maybe she'd actually go on a date with him. Then she remembered she was about to be richer, much richer, and would probably be out of the country for a while.

He'd agreed to the job, even though he'd only ever done drug deals and car thefts. At least that's what he said. Sold a few guns. Actually, a lot of guns. Bank robbery was new, but she had assured him it wasn't really a bank robbery, more like an office. No vault, no high-tech security system. Just scaring a bunch of white folks, which he assured her he excelled at.

Two hundred thousand dollars for him, and fifty for each of his guys. If they succeeded in ripping off Banke. She gave him ten thousand dollars out of her handbag.

"Damn, girl. Weren't you just selling me credit cards for five bucks a piece?"

She shrugged.

"I found someone who wanted to see this deal go down. He's got a good plan, and he's got seed money."

"This your Bonnie and Clyde dude?"

"That's him. So, you got at least ten grand even if the plan doesn't work."

"Suki, I make ten grand a week, this ain't nothing."

"Oh, then you can just give it back to me, if you don't want it."

He looked to make sure she was smiling when she said it, then smiled back.

"That's okay, I'll hold on to it."

Suki leaned over his desk and grabbed a pen and a piece of paper. He stood by the door, just watching.

She made a list and handed it to him.

"Five guys. This stuff. This address. Two o'clock. Come in one vehicle, big enough for eight people."

She started toward the door and he opened it for her, looking at the list as he did so.

"South Damen? Where the hell is this place?"

But she was already out of earshot, and in a few seconds, she was out the open garage door and into the beautiful sunshine, every guy in the place watching her go.

# 23

"Are we good?" Abby asked into the phone.

"Yes," said Eldon. "I've got just the person."

"I'd do it myself, but I don't want to be seen."

"It's no problem."

"Two forty-five."

"Got it. And Abby...you'll say goodbye to John for me?"

"I will."

"You're going to see him later, right?"

"Of course I am. What are you implying?"

"Nothing. Nothing at all. Be careful okay?"

"I've got to go."

Abby hung up, then called O'Brian.

"How's it going?" he asked.

"Just fine. I just wanted to say thanks again, for wiping down that school bus for us."

"Yeah, well, you think blowing up cars in the middle of downtown and joyriding school buses is maybe a little high-profile for your line of work?"

"Well, this is a big job, our biggest ever. We needed to make sure everyone was on board, and that little bit of excitement really helped the team gel. You did a great job."

"I almost didn't follow you when you took off across the grass."

"That was Suki, actually. I didn't know she had it in her."

"I worry about you guys sometimes. You're going to push it too far one of these days."

"That's why I'm calling."

"Uh-oh. Has it already happened? Do you need bail?"

"Ha ha. No, it's just that we'll be leaving town for a while after this one. I'm not sure when or if you'll hear from either of us again."

"Wow, Abby, that's...this is the big one, huh?"

"This is the big one."

"You've got my number if you need me."

"Actually, there is one more thing you can do."

"Name it. You know I owe you."

"We need a clean car. Something we can drive to Detroit. I've got international tickets out of Metro."

"You really are being careful. You think O'Hare's going to be looking for you?"

"I think a lot of things can go wrong, and I can count the number of people I trust on one hand."

"Well, I'm honored. And don't worry, I've got just what you need. Where do you want to pick it up?"

She gave him the address and hung up. She'd been sitting on an old, leather suitcase and now she stood up and took one last look around the apartment. They'd had it for over three years, the longest stretch they'd ever spent in one place. It was clean now, no trace of hair in drains, no fingerprints on the windows. Everything of sentimental value had already been put into a storage unit weeks ago.

She wandered over to the window and looked out across the lake. It was a beautiful day, and she could see windsurfers and sailboats dotting the water. She was going to miss Chicago; life was going to be very different for a while.

She absentmindedly reached up and traced her scar with her finger. Her life had changed drastically before, on a number of occasions. She would handle it again. In the suitcase was her make-up kit, which she would use to disguise her face, and a wig she would wear that matched the passport she'd be using.

She thought about her husband, uncertainty still gnawing at her nerves. Was this going to work? And what if it didn't?

She turned from the window and looked at the clock on the microwave. 12:20. Time to get going, she still had some loose ends to tie up, including getting a few thousand dollars from a bank account downtown. If the job blew up in their faces and they walked away with nothing, it'd be a good idea to have some traveling money.

John made plans, good plans. Even so, Abby made backup plans. That's just the people they were.

She crossed the room, picking up the suitcase on her way to the door. She took one last look around, then left, closing the door behind her, the keys dangling from the lock.

# 24

The Damen Silos stood on the edge of the river, defunct since the 1970s. Part of an industrial wasteland, they had become an enormous palate for graffiti artists. Concrete tunnels snaked out from beneath the towering silos, paint covering every available surface.

Eight people stood at the conjunction of two of the tunnels, a spot where there was no ceiling. The daylight streamed down from above to light the space.

John Adams finished drawing on the wall with a big piece of bright yellow chalk, stepped back and looked at the rest of the group.

Jacob Kirk stood nearby, dressed in a dark blue suit and tie, his tattoo hidden. He looked like he was ready for a business meeting. He felt strange being so dressed up in such a strange place.

Facing them were two men and two women, members of Dajuan's gang. They were dressed in black jeans and black T-shirts, black zip-up sweatshirts covering the guns held in their belts. The man named Dajuan was dressed the same, except he also wore several gold chains that stood out on his chest. It was a rookie mistake, but Adams wasn't going to make a big deal out of it.

Dajuan stood slightly apart, next to Suki, who wore her trademark leather jacket and boots. When Suki had come in with Dajuan, Adams had protested, strongly.

"I'm the getaway driver," Suki had said, with a pointed look that told him no argument was going to keep her out of this. He just shook his head and gave in. At this point, what could he do?

Adams looked around at the group and his eyes settled on Dajuan.

"Mr. Freeman?"

Dajuan snapped his attention away from Suki when he heard the formal address.

"Yeah. That's me."

Adams looked at him steadily.

"Mr. Freeman, you've met Mr. Kirk." He indicated Jacob. Dajuan nodded.

"You'll be in charge of your crew," Adams went on, "but Mr. Kirk will be in charge of you. Are you cool with that?"

"At your service, sir," said Dajuan. "I learned a long time ago that less ego leads to more money."

"I couldn't have said it better myself," said Adams. He turned to look at the others. "While I appreciate your cautious wardrobe, this is a daylight robbery, and we've got to get you into the building first. Do any of you have any other clothes with you?"

One of the women, African American with long straight hair raised her hand. "I've got a red jacket in the van."

"Excellent."

"I got a Bulls sweatshirt," said the guy named Jackie.

"That will work." He looked at the other woman, who was muscular, Caucasian, and had blonde hair in a ponytail. "Can you wear Suki's jacket?"

Suki gave him a look that would have cut stone, but took off her jacket and handed it to the woman, who went by the name Sandborn. He wasn't sure why Jackie used his first name and Sandborn used her last. Didn't matter.

"Okay," Adams continued. "That should do. We just have to get you into The Rookery and up to the third floor where Grafton Corp. has their offices. Jacob and I will already be inside. I'll go first, for my three o'clock

180

appointment with Lionel Banke."

He looked again at Suki.

"You cannot be seen."

"I told you, I'll be in the car."

"Okay. Jacob comes in a few minutes later, and while he's talking to the receptionist, the five of you will burst in and take over the place, taking Jacob hostage in the process. Declare that it's a robbery."

"But there's no money there, right?" asked Dajuan.

"No," interjected Jacob, "but there are bearer bonds in one of the secure rooms. It's not a safe, but we'll need a fingerprint from one of the partners to get in. Demand that a woman named Hendricks come out and open the door for you. She won't be there, we've arranged that, so then you'll demand Banke come out or you'll kill me. He opens the door, you and Jackie hustle Banke and I into the secure room. Once we are there, we'll make Banke show us where the bearer bonds are."

"What about you?" Dajuan asked, looking at Adams.

Adams turned around and pointed to the map of Grafton Corp. he had drawn on the cement wall.

"When Banke leaves me in the office, I'll go through this door here and down to the server room. I'll break in using a copy of Banke's fingerprint that Suki was able to acquire."

Kirk picked up the thread. "Then John will access their surveillance system and disable all the cameras and erase all the day's footage. When he comes out, we put all the staff into Banke's office and tell them we will shoot anyone who comes out. We take the bearer bonds, worth about five million dollars, and we leave calmly in pairs and rendezvous outside at the van."

Kirk conveniently left out the part where once in the server room, the phone gizmo would automatically start transferring millions of dollars into their private Swiss bank accounts. Dajuan would get his money and he'd be happy. Two hundred fifty thousand was a good score. Hell, a month or two ago, Kirk would have considered it the haul of a lifetime, but now his goals had grown exponentially.

Adams threw the piece of chalk up in the air and caught it.

"Any questions?"

Suki raised her hand. Adams looked at her with surprise.

"Yes?"

"I was just wondering, John, master planner," she said, her voice dripping with derision, "whether you've figured out yet that we aren't bringing you with us?"

There was a moment of absolute silence, and then Adams saw Kirk move in his peripheral vision. Pulling a pistol from the small of his back in one smooth move, he swung it toward Kirk but was too late. Kirk brought both fists down on Adams's wrist, as if he were chopping with an axe, and the gun fell from his grasp. Kirk stepped forward and leaned down, planting his shoulder into Adams's chest and driving him back into the cement wall. By the time Adams righted himself, Kirk had picked up the pistol and was aiming it at Adams's chest.

"Sorry, John," Kirk said, stepping backward until he was well out of Adams's reach.

Dajuan laughed, and his crew laughed along with him. He turned to Suki, but she had a serious look on her face, so he stopped.

"Okay, let's go," she said.

"Just a minute," Kirk said, staring at Adams with an undisguised sneer. "I want to savor this for a minute."

"Listen, Jacob..." John began.

"Shut up, okay, John? Just for a minute?" Kirk cocked the pistol. "I've heard enough of you, your advice, your criticism, your mysticisms, all your cisms. Christ, I don't know how Abby stands you, but I guess maybe she doesn't, huh? I notice she isn't here. In fact, I haven't seen her since yesterday at the bank."

"That's part of the—"

"Plan. Yes John, I understand. Everything is part of the plan. Well, was this? Huh? You saw this coming, right? Maybe you did. Maybe it was you who called the feds on my crew."

"No, I—"

"Maybe you thought that would put me out of it, but that worked just fine. Maybe you should've stopped calling Suki a kid and listened to her for a change, but no! You had all the answers. You had the plan. Well, what's the plan now? Someone swooping in to save you? Huh? I don't hear anyone coming."

He cupped his ear with his free hand, as if listening, and several of the others laughed, until the faint sound of an engine could be heard, growing louder from one of the tunnels that led off beneath the silos. Kirk's face changed.

"Oh, shit."

He turned his head for a minute and Adams lunged at him, both hands grabbing onto the gun which went off as he pulled it from Kirk's grip. A splash of red bloomed on Adams's chest as he crumpled to the ground, gun underneath him, coming to rest face down and motionless.

The echo of the shot caromed off the cement walls, mixed with Suki's scream and the growing sound of an engine.

Kirk stood still for half a second, then snapped out of it.

"Let's go. Everyone. NOW!"

Suki was still staring at Adams's motionless figure.

"Oh my god, oh my god, oh my god!"

Dajuan took her by the arm, attempting to pull her away.

"Come on, Suki. We've got to go."

Suki turned to yell at Kirk, who had already disappeared up the stairs toward the daylight and the van.

"This was NOT the deal! This was not..."

She broke off with a sob as Dajuan put his arm around her shoulder and ushered her away, moving her along quickly before she could look back again at the body in the dirt.

# 25

Adams waited for a thirty count after he heard Suki cry out, and then he exhaled heavily and rolled onto his back. Paintballs at close range don't tickle; he'd have sore ribs for a week. He sat up, then struggled to his feet. As the engine noise grew louder, echoing now in the cement tunnel, he bent down and picked up the paintball gun, tucking it back into his belt at the small of his back.

The noise was almost deafening now, and he turned to face it as a single headlight grew out of the darkness of the opposite tunnel, growing brighter and larger until a red motorcycle careened into the open area and skidded to a stop, the engine turning off.

The rider pulled off her helmet to reveal short red hair and an abundance of freckles.

"You John?" she asked.

"Who the hell are you?"

"I'm Batwoman. Eldon Shelby sent me here to take you wherever you need to go."

"Isn't it Batgirl?"

"I matured. My god, what have you got all over you? Is that ketchup? I thought I was a messy eater."

"It's paint."

"Even worse. Get on, but if you get any paint on my jacket, you're buying me a new one."

She was wearing a fitted black-leather jacket and blue jeans with a hardcore pair of leather boots. Adams pulled his suit coat shut over his paint-splattered shirt and buttoned it.

The bike was tiny, and he was worried that he would

throw the weight off, but he climbed on behind her.

"Where to?" she asked.

"The Rookery Building. It's on—"

"—LaSalle, I know."

"We need to get there in fifteen minutes."

"That's going to be difficult."

"It's imperative."

"Well, then, hang on tight. Sorry I didn't bring an extra helmet. You want mine?"

"No. I'll be fine."

"That's what you think," she said, and pulled the black helmet down over her face.

She started the engine and took off down the tunnel. Adams nearly fell off the back. He leaned forward and grabbed the woman around the waist. This was no time to be shy.

The little bike had more pep than Adams would have suspected, and in no time they were out of the tunnel and rocketing across the barren yard, completely in the wrong direction!

Adams tapped on the redhead's shoulder and pointed back toward the onramp to Route 55, but she just ignored him, swerving off the road and onto the little paved river walk that went around the Sun Times building. Two seconds later they were careening across traffic and turning left onto South Ashland and across the river, the redhead swerving around cars, passing anything in her way.

At the next big intersection, she went diagonally off the street and into another park, narrowly avoiding mothers taking their babies on an afternoon stroll. At one point she swung so hard around a kid with a ball that, with Adams's extra weight, they nearly overturned the motorcycle.

Suddenly, they were back out on a street, one that

Adams didn't recognize, but it ran diagonally across the regular gridded streets.

What Adams did recognize immediately was the sound of a police siren, noticeable even over the high-whining engine of the little motor bike. He looked over his shoulder and sure enough, they had a cop car on their tail. He took one hand off her waist just long enough to tap her on the shoulder and point behind them. She nodded and opened the throttle even more, causing Adams to clamp his hand back around her stomach. He thought they'd been going full speed before, but apparently not.

The sun flickered as they passed under the elevated train, still moving diagonally across the city, still being pursued by the cops. What they really needed was more traffic, something to get in the way of the police car but let the nimble little motorbike through.

The thought was barely in his head when the street they were on dead-ended at a cross street, but she kept right on going, directing the bike down a tree-lined driveway. Suddenly Adams was gawking at a football field as they crossed a clay track and then hurtled down a footpath and across a lawn.

Football field? Where the hell were they? He looked behind him and, as expected, the cop car was nowhere in sight. Why had he never gotten a motorcycle? It was brilliant.

They weaved through some more buildings, it was some kind of campus, and came out facing the Dan Ryan Expressway and the curling loops of the Route 290 on-ramps and off-ramps.

The woman jumped the curb again and headed down a grassy hill toward the highway.

"No!" Adams screamed. "No, no, no!"

But his words had no effect. They left the grassy berm

and passed under one of the on-ramps through a break in the guard wall that let them directly out onto Route 90, where the traffic, moving at seventy-five miles an hour, somehow failed to flatten the little fishtailing Honda as it moved perpendicularly across the lanes, through another break in the wall and then made a left so hard that Adams's knee scraped the pavement for a brief second before they righted themselves, crossed traffic again, and left the road to climb a small hill to the parking lot of an office supply store that let them out onto West Jackson.

Adams heard someone yelling "FUCK! FUCK! FUCK!" and then realized it was himself.

Thirty seconds later the bike pulled to a stop on La Salle, just in front of The Rookery Building. Adams climbed off slowly, looking down and noticing his pants were ripped and his knee was bleeding. The motorcycle driver flipped her visor up and looked at his leg.

"Sorry about that. You okay?"

"Okay? I could have been killed! You could have been killed!"

"Already dead," she said with a shrug. "You good?"

"Yeah," said Adams, still gasping from the adrenaline rushing through him. "I'm good."

She flicked her visor back down and sped off without another word.

Adams limped gingerly to the front door of the building, stepping through just as a big black van turned the corner up the block.

# 26

They entered the lobby of the building in pairs: Kirk and Dajuan, Sandborn and Jackie, the other two, whose names were Darnette and Flint. Kirk didn't know if Darnette was her first name or her last name and he didn't much care.

Dajuan's crew couldn't help but crane their necks to take in the marvelous details of the ornate space, but Kirk's attention was drawn completely to the woman standing on the balcony that ringed the lobby. He walked slowly up the grand staircase, the others in tow, and stopped in front of her.

"Abby," he said.

"Hello, Jacob." She took her sunglasses off so that they could look into each other's eyes.

"What are you doing here?" Kirk asked. His voice gave nothing away.

"Just making sure everything is going to plan." She looked at the others, raised an eyebrow. "I guess they'll do on short notice."

"Look, Abby. It's just about three o'clock. John's not coming. He lost his mind and we had to leave him. I'm sorry, but you know he's been erratic. I think it's the bipolar, but you would know best."

"But—"

"Don't interrupt. I can't talk now, I've got to get up there, I'm taking John's place with Banke. We're just going to bluff the rest."

"But John's here," said Abby, finally getting a word in.

Kirk stopped short.

"Abby, that's impossible."

"He told me to tell you to meet him for a second before you go up. He's right over there." She pointed at one of the retail storefronts on the balcony level. It was changing tenants and the front was covered with plywood, a door marked "No Admittance" set in the center.

"But Abby..."

She was already halfway down the stairs but stopped when he called her and turned back.

"I gotta go meet Suki, I promised her," she said before heading across the crowded lobby toward the door.

Kirk watched her go, and then turned again and looked at the door. He motioned Dajuan over to him.

"Have everybody wait right here."

"Man, it's almost three o'clock."

"Five minutes. Don't go anywhere."

\*\*\*

Kirk eased open the plywood door and stepped inside the dim room. There was no electricity, but windows, covered in thick plastic sheeting, let in light. He waited a moment for his eyes to adjust, then took another step into the room.

He took a deep breath, trying to calm his nerves. He'd been in high-pressure situations before, prided himself on keeping his cool. But this, he'd never had so much at stake. There was construction equipment lying about the room, and a large stack of drywall panels to one side of the mostly empty space.

"John?"

John Adams stepped from behind a pillar, gun straight out in his left hand, pointing at Kirk's head.

"Hello, Jacob. Take another step in please, to the middle of the room. Hands up."

Kirk did as he was told.

"I don't understand."

"Sure you do," said Adams. "You said it yourself. Plans and tricks. Tricks and plans. It's what I do." With his free hand he unbuttoned his suit coat to show his stained shirt. "It's a paintball gun."

Kirk let his arms drop.

"Jesus, John. What are you going to do, cover me with..." he trailed off as he realized being shot in the face with red paint would make it impossible for him to meet with Banke.

"Exactly," said John.

"How the hell did you beat us here. Helicopter?"

"I wish," said John, thinking of his knee and wincing involuntarily.

Kirk took a step closer, his hands still down at his sides. John stood his ground, the gun still pointed at Kirk's head.

"What do you want, John?"

"I want back in, same deal as before."

"That's ridiculous, John. I think we've broken the bond of trust."

"You've brok—"

"Ok, I've broken the bond of trust. I have to assume you'll try to screw me over at some point. I know I'd want revenge if you'd shot me and left me for dead."

"I want back in, or I cover you with paint and take your place. Why would you want nothing when you could have millions of dollars?"

"You cover me with paint, and I beat you to a pulp. Neither of us gets anything."

"You think you can beat me to a pulp?"

"I know I can. You've got your skills, I've got mine."

"Why would you want both of us to get nothing?"

"I. Don't. Trust. You."

Kurt didn't see how he could make it any plainer.

"All you have to do is be honest with me, finish the job, and you're a rich man. Just because you'd double-cross me doesn't mean that I'd double-cross you."

There was a loud and sudden ring as the phone in Kirk's pocket registered a call. They both jumped, and when Adams looked down toward Kirk's pocket, Kirk kicked hard and fast with his right leg, catching the gun and sending it flying across the room where it hit the floor and went off, causing an explosion of red against the freshly painted wall.

The phone rang again as the two men launched themselves at each other, going to the floor in a heap, both rolling away and jumping back to their feet, circling each other warily.

"You going to get that?" asked Adams and Kirk launched himself again. Adams sidestepped nimbly and tripped Kirk as he passed, causing him to sprawl on the floor.

Leaping to his feet, Kirk moved between Adams and the door and advanced, keeping his eyes on Adams's hips like he had learned in football practice a million years ago.

The phone stopped ringing.

Kirk attacked again, this time catching Adams's elbow when he tried to feint left, swinging him around and slamming him into one of the support pillars. Adams gasped and Kirk punched him in the kidney. Before Adams could move, Kirk grabbed him by the hair and slammed his face against the pillar. Adams kicked hard behind him and made contact with Kirk's shin, spun and kicked again as he did, higher, connecting with Kirk's hip and causing him to fall sideways onto his hands and knees next to a pile of tools.

Adams advanced, but Kirk grabbed a power drill and

threw it at Adams, keeping hold of one end of the cord. Adams got his forearm up in time to ward off the blow, but Kirk swung the drill around by the cord and whipped it into him again, this time catching him hard in the shoulder. He stepped forward and punched Adams in his already bleeding face, hitting him on the cheek bone and dropping him to the ground. He leapt on top of him, rolled him over, and pulled his arms behind his back, using the cord of the drill to tie his wrists. Then he stood up and kicked him hard in the ribs, three times, until Adams rolled over onto his back.

Adams groaned. His face was covered in blood, his arms were bent painfully underneath him.

"So," he gasped, spitting blood. "No deal, huh?"

Kirk almost laughed, but he was sick of this shit.

The phone rang again. Kirk pulled the big green phone out of his pocket.

"Who the fuck is calling this number."

"It's probably Suki, or Abby."

Kirk answered the phone.

"Yeah? I mean yes, hello...This is John Adams...Yes, I'm aware. In fact, I'm in the building...yes, it's just I have an injured leg and the elevator seems to be incapacitated. I'm taking the stairs, but it's slow going...that's right...I'll be there in five minutes."

He hung up.

"Nice one," said John, with a bloody grin. "Covered the leg and the sweat all in one."

Kirk looked down at his right hand. His knuckles were painful from punching John, but they weren't bleeding. He'd check with Dajuan before he went upstairs to make sure there wasn't any blood on his face. It was all going to work out just fine.

"I'm sorry, John, but I've got to go."

"You're not going to kill me?"

"I never planned to kill you. I don't like killing people. I was going to tie you up and leave you at the silos. You jumped at me and the gun went off. Police will find you here eventually. The bozos upstairs will wait until they're sure we're gone, then one of them will be brave enough to sneak to the phone and call 911. They'll search the whole building. By the time they find you I'll be in another country." He headed for the door. "Whereas you will spend a few decades in jail."

He eased the door open. Adams watched him go and then let his head fall back onto the floor.

# 27

"Ah, there you are Mr. Adams."

"Sorry for the delay, I really am."

Jacob Kirk hobbled across the lobby until he was leaning on the receptionist's desk. He was sweating slightly, and the woman worried about what the trouble with the elevator was. She'd call down in a few minutes and see what was going on. The building was lauded for its beauty and architectural significance, but it did have its issues.

"Oh please," she rose and stepped quickly to the water cooler. Kirk admired her figure. She was a little older than most receptionists—a lot of places like this made sure there was some young looker out front to get the old rich guys all excited—but she looked like the kind of woman who knew what she was doing. He worried briefly that she might have a panic alarm under her desk, but then he reminded himself that this was not actually a bank. Besides, Adams hadn't mentioned anything, and Kirk bet that if there was one, Adams would have known about it. That was the beauty of the betrayal: John had made a plan so smooth that it could run just fine without him.

Was he feeling guilty? No. He was not.

He watched as she filled a little paper cup and handed it to him. "With your injury, Mr. Adams, it's a shame you had to climb all those stairs."

As he reached for the cup, they both noticed white chalky dirt all along the side of his sleeve, from cuff to elbow. The receptionist tried in vain not to get caught looking. Had he fallen on the stairs? He smiled and set the cup on the desk so he could pat the dust and dirt away.

If he wasn't going to mention it, then neither was she. It would be impolite.

"The knee's an old football injury," Kirk told her. "Flares up every once in a while."

"Well," said the receptionist, "you and Mr. Banke will certainly have a lot to talk about."

"Oh yes," Kirk agreed. "I'm a huge fan. Never missed a game when I was a kid."

"I'll let Mr. Banke know you're here," she said, moving back behind the desk and picking up the phone.

Across the lobby a door opened, and Eleanor Hendricks emerged from her office, purse in hand.

"Jenny, I'm going down the street for a few minutes," she said. "Turns out there's a form that needs to be notarized by the end of the day."

Jenny waved in acknowledgement to Hendricks while speaking into the phone.

"That's right, he's here."

She hung up the phone as Hendricks exited into the hallway.

"You can go on in," Jenny told him. She gestured through an interior window, where Kirk could see a large open office space full of cubicles. A wide aisle ran down the middle, ending at a door on the far side. Beside the door was a window that looked into Banke's office, where Kirk could see the man stand up from his desk.

Jesus, thought Kirk, the guy really is a monster.

Banke spotted Kirk through the window and gave a big smile, gesturing to him with a massive hand. Jenny opened the connecting door and Kirk limped through, navigated the cubicles, and was met by Banke with a crushing handshake.

"Come in, come in," Banke boomed, stepping back to make way for Kirk.

"Thank you so much for rescheduling, having a little trouble with my knee. Old injury."

"No trouble. No trouble at all. Any friend of Mark Satterthwaite's is a friend of mine."

Kirk took a seat on one side of the massive, dark-stained wooden desk; Banke moved behind the desk and made himself comfortable in an oversized leather office chair. Kirk had no idea who Satterthwaite was, but if this went as planned, this conversation would be nice and short. In fact, when he looked through the window between Banke's office and the cubicle farm, he could see all the way down the open aisle they had just walked, through the receptionist's window, and into the lobby. As Banke launched into a description of Grafton Corp.'s best financial instruments, Kirk saw the lobby door open and Sandborn, one of Dajuan's group, enter the lobby. She was dressed in dark pants and a black shirt, with Suki's black leather jacket, the one with the gold studs. Her hair was pulled back, and she looked more or less presentable. It was her job to take on what had been Kirk's role, before he moved up to replace Adams. He watched her closely; it was possible that they would try to screw him over and run off with the bonds. That was fine, he thought, thinking of the big green phone in his suit coat pocket. In fact, that would be great. They would think they'd really pulled something over on Kirk, never knowing that tens of millions of dollars had been in their grasp.

Kirk had been listening to Banke talk, feigning attention, for several seconds.

"...derivatives instruments serve the primary purpose of hedging possible asset price fluctuation," said Banke, "if you see what I mean."

"Right," said Kirk, willing himself not to look back out

toward the lobby. "Hedge funds."

"Not quite," smiled Banke. "Let me explain it like this..."

***

The door to the offices of Grafton Corp burst open and two men and a woman rushed in, guns in hand. The first thought that leapt into Jenny's head was "brandishing." That's what they were doing with their guns. She was frozen where she stood. The other woman, who had just told Jenny that she was there to drop off a subpoena, turned and said, "What the—"

That was as far as she got before the black guy, long dreads and gold chains, put his arm around her neck, his elbow below her chin, and pointed his gun at her head.

"Hush now," he said.

The other guy, a white guy with a ponytail, pointed his gun at Jenny and said quietly: "Don't move, sweetheart." He moved around the desk and hustled Jenny away from the interior window so that no one in a cubicle would look up and see them.

The third intruder, a black woman in a red coat, crossed the lobby and stood in front of the door to the offices, a step back and to the side so that anyone coming through that door wouldn't know she was behind them until it was too late.

The guy with dreads moved to the side also, half dragging the courier with him.

"Let go of me!" the blonde gasped, trying to pull his arm off her windpipe.

"Hush, now," he said again, "or I am going to kill you and this woman, too." He nodded toward Jenny, who took an involuntary step back, only to find her movement blocked by the man directly behind her. She felt his hand on her shoulder and what had to be the end of a gun pushed into the small of her back. It was entirely possible that she was going to pee herself.

"What... what do you want?" Jenny's voice was shaking.

"I want you to pick up that phone," said Dajuan, pointing, "and call Eleanor Hendricks and ask her to come out here, because I have a gun and I'm thinking of using it."

"Ms. Hendricks isn't here," she said in a whisper.

"Then who's in charge?"

"Mr. Banke."

"Call him, then."

"You want Mr. Banke to come out here?"

"I do, and let him know that if he says anything to anyone between there and here, if he tries to call anyone, I'll kill you. My associate will be watching him cross the room. Any hesitation, any attempt to get help, you die. So," he grinned at her, "I suggest you be convincing."

\*\*\*

"Excuse me just a minute, John."

Banke reached out his oversized hand and picked up the receiver.

"I'm in a meeting, Jenny," he said sternly. He paused, and his face transformed from annoyance to surprise.

"Wait," he said, gasping. "What? Right now? I'll call the—"

Kirk watched Banke's face as the receptionist laid out the situation.

"I see, I'm not sure I can—"

Kirk raised his eyebrows in surprise. Was Banke going to chicken out and refuse to confront the thieves? That would be a detail even Adams wouldn't have guessed. The

199

sports hero, huddled in his office, hiding under his desk.

"Okay, I'll be right there. Tell them not to do anything rash."

He hung up the phone. Perspiration was rising on his forehead.

"Everything okay? You look like you've seen a ghost!"

Banke involuntarily looked through the office window. Kirk followed his gaze and could see Jenny standing at the matching window on the other side of the cubicle space, Jackie standing close behind her, his hand concealed behind her back. He raised his free hand and put his finger to his lips.

"What the hell is going on?" asked Kirk.

"I'm not sure." Banke stood and moved to the office door, stopping to look back at Kirk. "I don't want to alarm you, Mr. Adams. This is very unusual, but you'll have to excuse me for a minute. I think it's best if you stay here. I'll be right back."

"No problem," Kirk assured him, and watched as Banke exited the office and made his way toward Reception.

\*\*\*

John Adams lay on his stomach in the dirt and sawdust. Kirk had actually done a pretty good job with the electrical cord, he had knotted it at the wrists, then brought it up to tie it off at John's elbows, so that he was having a hell of a time reaching the knots.

He had been keeping time by counting Mississippis. He didn't think more than ten minutes had passed. No need to worry yet. The police wouldn't arrive for a while. Still, he certainly didn't want to be in the building when they did.

He could yell for help, and perhaps someone walking

along the balcony would have heard him, but that would be difficult to explain.

If he could have, he would have just walked out of there with his hands tied behind his back. Sure, someone may have tried to stop him, ask what was going on, but in John's experience most people didn't want to be involved, would simply look the other way. Unfortunately, Kirk had been smart enough to pull up his legs and tie them to the cord at his elbows, effectively hogtying him. Adams could have put up more of a fight, but it was important that Kirk stay on schedule.

He eyed the tool chest that sat on the other side of the room. It would be a pain, figuratively and literally, to roll all the way over there, but there was probably a box cutter or something like that in the chest.

He was preparing for the attempt when the door behind him opened. He tried to crane his neck to see. His elbows were tied so tightly he couldn't swivel his head. Whoever it was altered their trajectory to stay out of his line of vision; he heard their steps coming closer. If it was Dajuan or one of his crew come to finish him off, he was in trouble, he hadn't planned for that. He had been ninety percent sure Kirk wouldn't kill him, but Dajuan was an unknown quantity.

"Who's there?"

A hand grabbed the back of his skull, gripping his hair and forcing his head down toward the floor. Surprisingly, another hand grabbed his ass.

"Hello, Love." The hand moved down between his legs and cupped his crotch.

"Abby!"

"I got bored waiting outside," she said as she knelt beside him. "And I have to say, seeing you like this is oddly entertaining."

She squeezed.

"Could you stop that and untie me please?"

"You don't like it? I was thinking we could have a little fun here in this empty shop." She gave a little shiver. "It feels so transgressive."

"I promise you, Abby, as soon as we are on a tropical beach, watching the sunset, I will fuck you into next week. Repeatedly."

"Oooh. Big words from someone who can't get up off the floor. You promise?"

"I promise."

She stood and moved in front of him, squatting down so she could look into his face.

"No jobs for six months."

"There will be some loose en—"

"You know what I mean. Nothing new. Nothing dangerous. Nothing that puts stress on our relationship."

"I promise."

She ruffled his hair, moving from a squat to her knees, leaning over him to reach the knots. Her breasts grazed his head, and he breathed in deeply, smelling her familiar scent.

"Jesus, John, these are tight. Can you feel your fingers?"

"Only just. Try the tool box over there."

She stood and moved out of his sight. He heard her footfalls as she crossed the room, then suddenly the deafening sound of an electric rotary saw. It lasted only a moment, then whirred to a halt.

"Ah, no," he said hastily. "Terrible idea."

"I don't know, John, I think that would cut right through those cords."

"You're hilarious. Are we worried about time?"

"No," said Abby, walking back over to him. "I checked before I came looking for you, he hasn't even turned on the phone yet."

She knelt and used the box cutter she had found to cut carefully through the electrical cord.

John gasped and stretched his arms, then rolled over onto his back.

Abby stood up. "You look terrible," she said, reaching down to give him a hand up.

He took her hand and pulled hard, yanking her down on top of him where he lay, making her giggle as he drew her close, burying his head in her neck, breathing in deeply.

"You're going to make me cry," she warned him.

"*Lo siento.*"

They lay there for several minutes in the dim light.

\*\*\*

Suki sat in the getaway vehicle, drumming her fingers on the wheel. The sun was still shining, the sidewalks were full of people going about their business. From her spot at the curb she could see the side entrance of The Rookery Building, but there was no sign of life.

She looked at the dashboard. Jesus, never mind Bluetooth, this thing didn't even have a CD player. She rocked up on one hip so that she could pull her phone out of her back pocket. She thumbed it on so she could see the time. It was 3:15 pm. Another 30 minutes to wait. She was hungry. Too bad there weren't any hotdog stands around here. She wondered if Maltini's Pizza would deliver to a parked car. Nah, they probably couldn't deliver in time. She set the timer on her phone for 25 minutes, then set it on the passenger's seat, and looked at the side door again. Started the car to make sure it still worked—you never know—and it did. She wasn't usually this nervous. She drummed her fingers on the wheel...

Lionel Banke opened the door and entered the lobby, his eyes searching out and fixing on Jenny Stevens. She'd worked for Grafton longer than he had, and was a nice woman, if a bit exacting, though he supposed that was a good quality in a receptionist.

She met his look with barely controlled panic, and he felt something hard poking into his kidneys as the door swung closed behind him. He tensed up.

"Take it easy, big fella," said a woman's voice from behind him. "We're just interested in your index finger. Don't mind leaving the rest of you in a bloody heap on the floor. Other hand, don't give us any shit and we'll be out of here in fifteen minutes, and you and Miss T.J. Maxx here will be just fine."

Jenny involuntarily looked down at her work outfit, which was sensible yet slightly feminine. It seemed she was being insulted, but frankly she was too scared to worry about it.

"Ain't your money anyway," said Dajuan. "Well, maybe some of it. But you got insurance, yeah?"

"What exactly do you want?" Banke kept his big voice soft. "This isn't a bank; we don't have any money here."

Dajuan still had his arm slung loosely around Sandborn's throat. He could afford to be lax because, of course, she was on his side. With his gun he pointed to a door on the other side of the room.

"We want to go down there, now, before anyone pokes their head in here and causes me to shoot this lady."

He motioned again, and Jackie and Darnette began herding Lionel and Jenny toward the side door that led to the bearer bonds. Just as they opened it and were ushering their captives through, the door to the outside hallway opened.

It was Flint, the fifth member of Dajuan's crew.

"Jesus, man," hissed Dajuan. "You scared the shit outta me. What the fuck are you doing?"

"Just making sure everything's cool."

"Of course everything's cool, 'cept for my lookout man ain't looking out. Get your ass back out there. Make sure we see anything coming at us long before it gets here."

"It's really quiet," said Flint.

"I'm sorry if you're bored. I'll let you torture the white lady after if you want."

Jenny's already pale face grew paler, and she slumped slightly against Jackie, who squeezed her upper arm hard and pushed her through the door and down the hall.

"Don't worry," Jackie whispered to her, "he's just kidding. We only take the young ones."

Jenny began to cry, but kept moving forward, focusing on the head and shoulders of Lionel Banke as he led them down the hallway. He was enormous, and the woman behind him seemed tiny in comparison. Except, of course, she had a gun. If anyone could help in a situation like this, it would be Lionel. The Grafton brothers, both selfish, old men, would have probably stroked out on the spot.

Jenny heard the door shut behind her and looked back to see the man with dreadlocks following her down the hall. She didn't know what had happened to the courier woman. She hadn't heard a gunshot, so she didn't think she was dead. Maybe she was with that other black guy.

The little parade came to a halt at the end of the hallway, at a solid metal door that led to the records room.

"Okay, big man," said Dajuan, pointing his gun at Banke. "Open it up, yeah?"

Lionel Banke assessed the situation. Like being a running back and being handed the ball. How many defenders? How much open space? Football players were good at physics. The woman behind him had a gun. The prick with the ponytail was using Jenny as a shield, and he had a gun, too. The guy with dreads was standing ten feet back, also with a gun. Even in his prime, Banke couldn't have covered that distance quickly enough.

He sighed. Turning back to the door, he reached his hand out to the little black square mounted on the wall and pressed his thumb to it. There was a click, and he turned the handle and pulled the door open, stepping back and out of the way.

"Good man," said Dajuan. "Good choice."

"No need for anyone to get hurt," said Banke. "It's just rich people's money."

"Not for long," Dajuan grinned. "J-man, you go in first, then I'll send him in. You keep him covered."

"C'mon baby," said Jackie, pushing Jenny ahead. Dajuan was young, but he had a good grasp of tactics, and he knew not to take Banke at his word. The guy, even at his age, could probably crush Dajuan's skull with his bare hands. He wasn't letting his guard down, and he wasn't letting Banke within ten feet of him or Jackie. He'd shoot him if he had to.

He motioned to Banke with the gun, and Banke went into the room, where Jackie motioned him up against the side wall. Then, apparently tiring of his human shield, he pushed Jenny across the room at Banke. She clung to him and let a sob escape as she pushed her face into his chest. She'd kept it together so far, but now she started crying freely.

"Okay, man," said Dajuan, looking at Banke. "Let's make this quick so there's no time for things to get complicated. Simple, quick, nobody hurt. You got me?"

"What is it you want?" asked Banke.

"Bearer bonds. We know they're in here. Where?"

The room held a six-foot wooden table and two chairs. A nice light hung over the table, but there were fluorescents recessed in the ceiling as well. Jackie stood on one side of the table, pointing his gun across at Banke and Jenny, who stood against a blank wall. The wall at the far end of the room was covered with heavy-duty filing cabinets. There were no windows, and no other door besides the one they entered. Dajuan had closed the door behind him and now stood leaning against it, well back from Banke.

Lionel Banke considered his options, considered the smug Grafton brothers who just treated him like a show piece, and came to a quick decision. He pointed across the room.

"It's that double-size one, on the end."

Jackie walked over to the wall of file cabinets.

"This one?"

"No, one over, the double-wide one."

"This one?"

"Yes."

Jackie grabbed the handle and pulled, but the drawer wouldn't open. He pulled again, hard, but it didn't give. He looked at Dajuan.

"Locked."

"You think?" said Dajuan.

"Hey man, don't get mad at me!"

"Mr. Banke," said Dajuan, turning his attention back.

"My keys are back in my office."

"Excellent. Just excellent. How about you, lady?"

Jenny had gotten her breath back and was standing next to Banke now, wiping her eyes on her sleeve.

"I don't have keys to anything in here. Only the officers."

"Should we call you know who?" said Jackie. "He's in this guy's office."

"Shut up, dude," Dajuan said quickly, but it was too late. He looked at Banke and could tell by his expression that the man had just realized Jackie was talking about Kirk, who was supposed to be an innocent bystander. Oh well, that would be Kirk's problem.

Dajuan turned back to Jackie.

"Break the lock, dude."

Jackie turned back to the drawer, pulled hard again. He set his gun on the table and tried again with both hands. Banke eyed the gun, but Dajaun was watching him closely.

Jackie straightened up and turned back to Dajuan.

"Maybe we shouldn't have shot the professional thief, huh?"

"Just break it open," Dajuan said through clenched teeth.

Jackie shrugged, picked up his gun and turned back to the drawer.

"No!" shouted Dajuan, but his voice was drowned out by the deafening report of Jackie's pistol in the enclosed space.

***

Richter and another man approached the vehicle. The windows were down, and a brown arm lay lazily along the driver's door.

"Miss Adams, hello."

Suki turned and took them in, removing her sunglasses to do so. The man with Richter was well built, with close-cropped hair and blue eyes. He had on a black FBI windbreaker.

"Hey there," she said.

"This is Agent Caleb Carter, of the FBI," said Richter.

Carter squinted his eyes with skepticism.

"This is your source? What is she, sixteen?"

Suki nonchalantly raised her hand and gave him the finger.

"Are you even old enough to drive?"

"Yeah, man, but I have to tie these blocks of wood to my feet with some old rope. It's a drag."

Carter actually smiled. Maybe he wasn't so bad after all.

"Her intel was good on the carwash gang," said Richter, "even if her story was rubbish."

"Rubbish?"

Suki looked offended.

"It strains credibility that you alert us to criminal activity in Ravenswood in the morning, and then by afternoon you have also uncovered a massive conspiracy to rob the Grafton Corporation."

Suki shrugged.

"The info this morning was good, wasn't it?"

"It was. We've been after a few of those guys for a while. We found enough drugs at the carwash to put them away for a good long time."

"The info is good now, too. There's an armed robbery taking place up there right now. Are you interested in it, or are you interested in me?"

"Both." Carter looked up at the windows of The Rookery, then back at Suki. "Gangs, robbers, how is it you know so many fine people, Miss Adams?"

"It's Chicago."

Carter nodded as if that explained everything. "Armed, you say?"

"Definitely."

"We're going to clear the entire first two floors," said Richter, "quietly as we can. That's a big job, going to inconvenience a lot of people."

"Alex," said Suki, looking at Richter, "I'm sure."

Carter grinned and turned to the detective. "Alex, huh?"

Suki picked a photograph up off the dashboard and handed it to Carter. It was a of Kirk sitting on a bench in a park, eating a piece of pizza.

"Well, he looks familiar," said Richter.

"You missed him this morning at the car wash."

"Better call Levesque," said Carter, then glanced again at the photo. "Doesn't look like a mastermind of white-collar crime."

"He'll be in a blue suit."

"Oh, well then..."

Richter looked at Carter. "Are we good?"

"Yeah. Let's do it. It'll be on your head if it's a false alarm, though."

"Great."

"Did you try calling up to Grafton?"

"I did, repeatedly, no answer. I called one of the Grafton brothers. He's worried. Says someone should be answering the phone."

"All right. We better move quickly, then."

Carter walked off without another word or glance at Suki, pulling his phone from his pocket and initiating a call. By the time he reached the corner of the building, several black SUVs were pulling up, disgorging men in dark suits.

Richter looked back at Suki.

"I don't know whether to thank you or detain you."

"You're welcome," she smiled.

"I think you better stay here. There's a lot of unanswered questions."

"I will, I will. I want to see what happens." She nodded toward the corner of the building. "You better get going or you're going to miss all the fun."

He squared his shoulders and headed off briskly.

Suki put her sunglasses back on and picked up her phone from the passenger's seat. She watched it closely, waiting for the signal, and when it came, she made a call.

"Hi, Jacob. It's Suki."

***

John Adams leaned heavily on his wife. This day had taken a lot out of him. He had cleaned up his face in the bathroom as best he could, then they had descended to the lobby, and were now being ushered out by FBI agents, along with everyone else on the first and second floor of the building.

He marveled at how quietly and efficiently it was being done. Everyone was funneled toward the front door, where an agent asked to see their driver's licenses, and gave each person a quick pat-down. Adams had been sure to leave his paintball pistol in the trash in the bathroom.

They queued in a short line, just as a man in the doorway began to complain. He looked like a stock broker or a financial analyst. Nice suit, slick haircut, fashionable stubble, shitty attitude.

"Listen dude," he was saying to the officer at the door. "I don't know what your game is, but this is a total violation of my rights. I don't have to show you anything."

"That's right," said another agent, stepping up to the man. "I'm excited to discuss this with you, but why don't we move over here so that everyone else can make a quick and orderly exit. They'd all like to go home now."

"I'd like to go home now, too," said the man as he was led off to the side.

"Well, I'm afraid that ship has sailed," said the agent as he led the man away.

Adams smiled.

Abby had a more serious look on her face.

"What is it?" asked John.

"Hendricks, right outside the door."

John looked past the people at the entrance and could see Eleanor Hendricks outside on the sidewalk, craning to get a look in and see what was going on. He looked back at the red-headed Abby.

"Weren't you a blonde that day? I think you'll be fine."

"I hope so."

"She's way too interested in what the FBI are doing to recognize you."

"Maybe we should have worn our pirate and pigeon disguises."

"That should be the name of a law firm, Pirate and Pigeon."

"Or a series of children's books. Maybe that's what I'll do next."

The agent at the door checked their driver's licenses, jotted down their names, took their phone numbers, and then asked them to submit to a quick pat down. They did, and seconds later emerged into the late afternoon sunlight that was slicing between the towering buildings. Arm in arm, they walked past Eleanor Hendricks and strolled to the corner, where John came to an abrupt halt.

"What?" Abby looked around quickly.

Half a block away was the big black van that had brought Suki, Jacob, and Dajuan's crew to The Rookery. It was surrounded by uniformed police, and yelling and gesturing at the officers was Madeleine Levesque in her sharp, grey pantsuit and dark sunglasses.

"Damn," hissed Abby. "Damn, damn, damn."

"It's okay," said John, steering her away from the scene and toward a side alley. "I'm sure Suki'ss not in there." He looked up and down the street. "Do you see our getaway car anywhere?"

Abby searched the line of parked cars.

"There!"

It was an old Galaxie 500.

"Jesus, Abby, that's a beautiful car."

"Danny lent it to us."

"Meaning we have to give it back?"

"Yes. We'll be on a plane soon, remember?"

"*Si*. Of course."

Still, Adams looked lovingly at the old car as he limped slowly toward it.

***

The moment Banke left his office, Kirk began to sweat. This was it, game time. He watched through the window as the ex-football star made his way across the room of cubicles, making sure the man said nothing to anyone along the way. As it was, because it was Friday afternoon, there were only a few people still working, and none of them looked up as Banke walked by.

As soon as Banke passed through the far door and into the reception area, Kirk leapt from his seat and left the office. Turning right, he walked along the wall until he reached the far corner of the room and a large door of dark wood. There was metal plating along the edge of the door and a substantial brass handle. To the left of the door was a black rectangle with a little red light glowing. Kirk reached into his interior suit pocket and pulled out latex gloves and the glasses case. He took a quick look over his shoulder to make sure no one was watching, then pulled on the thin gloves. Inside the case was a short stick with a round piece of pink rubber on the end, wrapped in plastic like a lollipop. Carefully, Kirk unwrapped the plastic and let it fall to the floor. Holding only the stick end, he pressed the rubber end against the black square of glass that was set within the black metal rectangle next to the door. Nothing happened.

Kirk waited until the count of three, then flipped the thingamajig over and pushed the other side against the scanner. There was a quiet beep and the red light turned green. He smiled and turned the big brass handle. The door opened smoothly, and he passed through it and down the long hallway beyond. The left-hand wall had evenly spaced windows, letting in the afternoon glow. The right-hand wall had several unmarked doors in a row. He walked the length of the hall, about fifty feet, to where the doors gave way to windows that looked into a large, dim room full of racks and racks of computer equipment. Kirk marveled. This was the other side of the world from the little local bank they had been in yesterday. This looked more like his idea of Silicon Valley or a scene from Mission Impossible.

He grinned. This really was like Mission Impossible, and he was pulling it off. He was fucking Tom Cruise, and it felt good. Wait till the guys at the car wash heard about this.

His face darkened, realizing that was all gone now. Everything he had built. He shrugged it off. New life now. Keep moving forward.

At the end of the hall were two doors. One straight ahead, the other on the right. That one led into the server room and had not only a fingerprint console but also a deadbolt. Kirk didn't have a key, but he wasn't worried. Adams had known access to the server room would be limited. Keeps the servers safe, dust-free, and climate-controlled. The device only had to be within fifty feet. Adams was a clever bastard, Kirk would admit that.

He looked through the window at the servers. He was close enough. This would do fine. He turned to the other door. Better make sure no one would surprise him. It, too, had a fingerprint scanner, and the light turned green when he tried Banke's fingerprint on it. He opened the door just far enough to poke his head in and look around.

Filing cabinets, a table and two chairs, and set into the wall on the opposite side of the room, a floor-to-ceiling safe. Kirk stepped into the room and whistled. He closed the door behind him and crossed to the safe, putting the lollipop back in his pocket. Now this was a proper bank heist. The door was three-and-a-half feet wide, polished steel, with a classic black dial set dead center. Next to the handle was one of those little metal steering wheels, just like you see in the movies. Kirk rested his gloved hand on it and imagined twirling it open, the door swinging smoothly back to reveal bars of gold in great tall stacks.

He laughed and shook his head. It was probably full of stacks of paper. Old wills and testaments. Dirty secrets. As alluring as it was, it wasn't holding fifty million dollars. No, that was behind him, on the other side of that wall, in the banks of servers. It was time to get going. He didn't want Dajuan getting restless, doing something stupid. Kirk was supposed to be erasing security video tape, that's what Dajuan thought. He couldn't take too long.

He pulled out a chair and sat down, took the big green phone out of his pocket and placed it face up on the table, pushed the home button to bring it to life. The screen lit up, a round circle in the middle, and above it the words: "Press thumb to circle."

Fuck. That hadn't been there before! What had John done? Was it a fingerprint passcode? Had he made it so that only Adams could operate it? If so, he was fucked. All this for nothing! He thought briefly about going back down to the second floor where Adams was lying tied up. He'd take a box cutter and cut his fucking thumb off. That'd show him for being an asshole.

Deep breath. Deep breath. Try it anyway, maybe it was

a dummy. If it didn't work, there was still time to go back downstairs. He pressed his thumb to the circle. Nothing. He waited three seconds, five, ten.

Damn it, the glove! He stripped it off his right hand and tossed it on the table, looked back at the phone and gingerly placed his thumb on the circle again. The phone beeped, and the screen turned white. Kirk pulled his thumb away. Words scrolled across the screen.

Greetings Jacob Vaclav Kirk. Print accepted and transmitted.

Thank Christ!

The white screen dissolved, and the home screen appeared. Kirk scrolled to the right until he found the Banke Account App and pushed the button. Just as he did, the green phone rang, loudly, with the sound of an old-time, rotary phone, bright and blaring.

Kirk all but had a heart attack. He leapt up, the chair overturning behind him and falling to the floor. The phone rang again, and Kirk snatched it up. The screen was now black except for the words, Incoming call, and a little green circle underneath them.

He punched the home button again, trying to get back to the app, but nothing happened except the phone rang again. Kirk looked at the door, wild-eyed, expecting the noise to bring someone running. There seemed to be no way to turn it off without answering the call so, reluctantly, he pushed the green button.

"Hi Jacob. It's Suki."

"Not now Suki, I'm right in the middle of it!"

"You sure are," she said with a laugh.

"I'm serious, I've got to start the transfer."

"Oh, don't worry about that. Abby started it remotely over an hour ago."

"What? But I've got the phone."

"Yeah. She used some other device. Planted it in the

server room over a week ago."

Kirk ran his palm over his bald head. None of this was making any sense. The last few days tumbled through his brain, looking for something to latch on to. Had Suki double-crossed him, pretending to double-cross John? Or was she working with Abby? Had Abby left John?

"What the fuck is going on, Suki? What have you done? We had a deal."

"And I'm really sorry about that, Jacob."

"You made a deal with Abby."

"Years ago. Oh, here they come now, finally. God, John looks terrible, what did you do to him?"

Kirk leaned on the table with one hand, the other holding the phone to his ear. He was afraid he was going to start hyperventilating. The room had gotten hot. There was sweat on his forehead.

"Years? What do you mean years? You hired us to get money from your dad!"

"Oh no. That wasn't me. That was Lionel Banke's daughter."

"You're Lionel Banke's daughter!"

"Nope."

"But you got the fingerprint!"

"No, that was Chantal Williams. Lionel Banke's illegitimate daughter. Our client."

"Quit fucking with me and tell me what's going on!"

"Temper, pal. You're going to have an aneurism. Here are my folks, I'll let them explain."

"Suki!" Kirk shouted into the phone, no longer caring if anyone heard him.

He heard a car door open and some rustling.

"Hey, Wart," said John's voice. Shit! How did he get untied?

"Don't call me that," said Suki. "You know I hate that!"

"I can't help it, I'm in a great mood."

217

"You look like shit," she retorted.

"Hey Jacob," said a bright voice. "It's Abby. You're on speaker phone. How's it going up there?"

"What have you done, you bitch?"

"Hey, hey!" came John's voice. "Watch it."

"How...I don't... What the fuck?"

"It's simple," said Abby.

"It's actually pretty complicated," said John.

"I'm afraid you've been set up, Jacob," Abby continued. "That device isn't going to work for you. In fact, it just transmitted your fingerprint to Agent Caleb Carter of the FBI."

"You're bluffing. If you didn't need to get the device close to the servers, then why was John going to all the trouble to come up here?"

"He wasn't. He knew you'd double-cross him."

"Bullshit!"

"*Si*, it's true," said John. "But I wanted to give you the chance to not do it, to follow my plan. Right up to the end I gave you the chance to not betray me. If you'd have stuck with me, I'd have made some excuse to the client and let you get away."

"Client? What client?"

"Marion Menard. You broke into her house in June, and she took it very, very personally. She hired us to make sure you spent at least twenty years in jail. She wanted us to kill you, but I let her know in no uncertain terms that we don't kill people."

"I'd do it!" said Suki.

"Yes," said John, "you probably would. We've raised you poorly."

"Wait a minute," gasped Kirk. "Suki's your—"

"Our daughter, yes. She sometimes does jobs with us."

Kirk was stunned.

"Why would you bother coming here? Confronting me

218

at all if this was all a setup?"

"It sounds crazy, Jacob," said John, "but we actually liked you. And we don't like Marion Menard so much. We regretted taking that job, so we thought we'd give you a chance to get out of it by helping us with this one. You're only taking the fall because you betrayed us."

He'd been played. Played from the beginning. His mind reeled as he considered it. The card game. The guy in Oz Park. The aquarium? Everything was a big fucking question mark.

"Ethan Allen?"

"Now you're getting there," said John. "He's our friend with the connections."

Of course. Wasn't there some furniture company named Ethan Allen?

Furniture...

"Old man Shelby! The mobster with the furniture company! That's how you were able to get me off the hook with Catalano!"

"And see the thanks we get!" said Abby. "Anyway, this has been fun, but we've got to get out of the country now. Vacation time for us. Say hello to Agent Carter. He should be up to see you any minute."

The phone went dead.

Kirk stood still a moment longer, then he threw the phone across the room with every ounce of strength he had. It hit the unmoving face of the vault and shattered.

Well, fuck them. He wasn't out of this yet. There were still the bearer bonds, and he had a few tricks up his own sleeve.

Moving quickly now, Kirk removed his suit coat. From an inside pocket, he pulled a small clump of hair which he unrolled to reveal a black toupee. He oriented it and then pulled it tight over his head. Also from the inside pocket of the jacket he pulled a pair of glasses with dark blue, plastic frames. He threw the suit coat in the corner and looked around for a mirror, but there wasn't one. No matter. The disguise wouldn't have to last long. If they thought he would just—

His internal rant was interrupted by the unmistakable sound of a gunshot.

# 28

Kirk raced down the hall and burst through the door into the open office space. Workers had heard the sound, too, and were standing in their cubicles looking at each other with curiosity. He careened past them and pushed through the door to the lobby.

Flint and Sandborn were in a heated discussion by the door to the outer hallway.

"Where the fuck!?" was all Kirk could get out.

Sandborn pointed to the other door, and Kirk sprinted through it and down the hallway.

\*\*\*

The gunshot echoed through the room.

"What the fuck is wrong with you?" Dajuan said loudly, his ears ringing.

"What? You wanted it open, ri—"

He was interrupted by Lionel Banke, who took one massive stride to cross the room and leap onto Jackie, grabbing down hard on his gun hand as they collapsed in a heap.

Jenny screamed, and Dajuan took two steps into the room toward her when he saw Lionel Banke wrest the gun from Jackie and start to stand.

Dajuan made a quick mental calculation that involved shooting a famous black man in the back, decided to fuck that, and turned and yanked open the door that led back to the hallway.

The door opened to reveal a dark-haired white man,

running at him full tilt. He made no calculation at all, just raised his gun and fired, shooting the disguised Kirk square in the chest. In the confined space the noise was overwhelming. The victim's momentum was such that he crashed straight into Dajuan, knocking them both down as blood spurted against the mauve colored wall.

Dajuan looked up from where he lay on his back, on the floor, to see Lionel Banke standing above him, pointing Jackie's gun at his face. After a moment, the ringing in his ears cleared enough that he could hear the shouts of men in the lobby, and, in the distance, sirens.

***

The Galaxie 500 pulled away from the curb and began a journey that would take it out of the city, across Indiana and into Michigan.

"If it makes it that far," snorted Suki.

"What are you talking about?" asked John, an incredulous look on his face. "This is a beautiful car."

"It doesn't even have a fucking CD player."

"Language," warned Abby.

"You know the job's over now, right?" asked John. "You can drop the act of being annoying and angry."

"Yeah, whatever," said Suki, but she smiled up at them in the rearview mirror. "They'll catch him, right?"

"They'll catch all of them," said John, "thanks to you. You do good work."

"We've really missed you," added Abby.

Suki could see that the two of them were holding hands in the back seat, and she felt her heart swell.

"It was a brilliant plan," she said. "Fulfilling one job by using the target to carry out another job. It's like killing two birds with one of the birds."

"Four birds, actually," said Abby.

"Four?"

"A man named Edward Bowker hired us to take care of a card cheat named Stephen Brock. Marion Menard hired us to take care of Jacob Kirk. Chantal Williams hired us to steal three million dollars from Lionel Banke, and Eldon Shelby hired us to get rid of Dajuan's gang. He and his uncle are on this kick to stop some of the city's rampant gun violence. Apparently, your boyfriend Dajuan was one of the big players."

"Boyfriend, ha! Very funny."

She turned the ancient car on to Route 90. She wasn't sure she'd be able to get it up to seventy miles per hour.

"Oh, and don't forget, I got to punch Lieutenant Levesque in the face." Abby's voice was full of glee.

John turned and looked at his beautiful wife. His devious, violent, beautiful wife.

"*Si*, my love, and now we have no more jobs. Just as I promised. Just relaxation and figuring out how best to distribute a vast amount of money."

Suki, who had been fiddling with the AM radio—the only thing the car had—stopped, the sultry sounds of "Girl from Ipanema" coming from the tinny speakers.

"How vast, exactly?" she asked.

"Sixty-two million dollars," said Abby.

John smiled and exhaled.

It felt like he had been holding his breath for weeks.

Behind him, the sun was getting low. Ahead of him, the majesty of Gary, Indiana loomed. He'd miss Chicago, but Europe would be nice. He'd never actually been.

The relief in his chest was so palpable that he began to laugh, and he squeezed Abby's hand as she began to laugh, also.

Suki shook her head like they were crazy, but she was smiling                                                                    too.

The End

The Levelers will return in:

**The
Train
Job**

www.stephanieandrewsauthor.com